THE COST OF VICTORY

After dinner, Tito watched Luke ride off toward his own place, on the opposite side of the Dakota Creek. For a time, he remained standing in the dark. He wondered how many more nights he could enjoy the serenity of the evening. Puggot was certain to find out he worked for Wells Fargo—it had come out at his hearing in Ivory Flats. He would follow his trail back to Broken Spoke and come looking for him. There was no escaping the inevitable. It nagged at his conscience that he might have been better off to stay at Fallwood or Ivory Flats and face the man and his guns. The odds would not have been good, but he would not be risking the lives of his friends.

They were all good, honest men. With the support of these men and their guns, he could beat Puggot.

But at what cost? he wondered. How many of them would be killed or wounded?

DESTINY AT BROKEN SPOKE

Terrell L. Bowers

LEISURE BOOKS NEW YORK CITY

Especially for Marcia Markland,
who suggested a Broken Spoke series.

A LEISURE BOOK®

June 2006

Published by

Dorchester Publishing Co., Inc.
200 Madison Avenue
New York, NY 10016

Copyright © 1998 by Terrell L. Bowers
Published in hardcover by Avalon Books.

ISBN 0-8439-5715-8

The name "Leisure Books" and the stylized "L" with design are trademarks of Dorchester Publishing Co., Inc.

Printed in the United States of America.

DESTINY AT
BROKEN SPOKE

Chapter One

The early October sun should have felt good, but it seemed to scorch Hermando Lopez's body like over-cooked bacon. He squirmed helplessly from the searing heat and pulled the cap from his canteen. Shutting his eyes against the relentless rays of the blinding sun, he tipped it high and pressed it to his parched lips, desperately seeking even a single drop of moisture.

Nothing.

Despondent, he angrily tossed it away and cursed under his breath. No water, no food, no one in sight for miles. How long had he been lying on the desert floor? A day? Two days?

"Hey, out there!" he yelled hoarsely, "Can anyone hear me?"

Nothing.

"I need help!" he tried again. Then he strained his ears, listening, praying someone could hear his cries.

Still nothing.

Several magpies had gathered, like turkey buzzards, drawn by the carcass of Hermando's dead horse. He had attempted to kill a couple of the miserable scavengers, each time they landed on or near the animal, but now his ammo was spent. They still flew off each time he yelled out, but his voice was about gone. He lay next to a sprawling mescal, but he was opposite the leeward side now, exposed to the sun. He wiped his beaded brow with the back of his hand. He knew it was not the heat from the sun, but fever from the infection and bleeding of his own broken leg that pumped fire through his body.

The world before his burning eyes was distorted and unreal, lost in an ocean of heat waves. He groaned, ravaged by the elements, his strength waning, his mettle nearly spent, and cursed his luck. He'd been going to make a better life for his family, get them a real home. All it would have taken was a bit of luck. He could have doubled his meager stake, when he bet on a horse race. It was so close, it almost worked—if only the nag had not stumbled at the very end.

Run like my own knock-kneed, clumsy, good-for-nothing-but-dog-meat mount!

There was the flutter of wings and Hermando rotated his head enough to see one of the camp robbers land a few feet away. It did an awkward sort of dance as it hopped over to the dead animal. A second bird followed a minute later.

"Git!" he rasped. "G'wan! Git!"

But the birds paid him no attention. They were growing bolder, no longer afraid of his harmless threats.

I'll be next on your menu, Hermando lamented inwardly, realizing he should have saved a bullet for himself. What if the birds decided to start on him, once he grew too weak to move? Would they eat him alive? He glowered at the black-and-white creatures and grated hoarsely, "Hope you ugly, black-hearted chickens choke on me!"

He lifted up his eyes and stared skyward. The incredible ache in his head made it feel as if his brain was expanding, pressed too tightly against his skull, about to explode! His vision was growing worse. Everything was blurred before his eyes, yet he could tell that dusk was only a couple hours away. There were a half-dozen of the scavengers now, scattered on or near the horse carcass. His own end was near. Soon, he would become a meal for some of Nature's vultures. Twisting around, he attempted to see the mountains off to the west. It would be a final treat to at least look upon his last sunset.

Regret flooded through his body as he again closed his eyes. In a voice that was a mere whisper, he prayed, "Mary, Mother of God, please watch over my children." His voice cracked on the words. "Forgive me for not being a very good father. You look after them, would You, please? They deserve much more than I ever gave them."

He had to stop, sobbing inwardly at the notion that he would never see their faces again, never hold one of them in his arms. *I should have been a better provider,* he thought. *I should have given them a decent home. If only things had worked out different.*

The deadly fever ravaged his thinking. He could no longer control the agony. Rolling his head back and forth, he sought relief of both physical and mental anguish. As the sun slowly sank over the hills, his own life's energy drained into the dusk. Hermando Lopez was beset with a blackness, a dark world that beckoned him to succumb. Knowing resistance was futile, he let the endless void engulf him. The pain slowly subsided.

Then nothing.

* * *

Although Tito Pacheco had the knowledge and skill to have made a living at games of chance, he didn't play cards often. When between trips for Wells Fargo, or when he was bored, he used the game to socialize or pass the time. He was enjoying his new position for Wells Fargo, that of a field operator, a man designated to travel to new locations and set up way stations. With the company growing larger every year, there was always a new locale to be added to their delivery route, another region to be mapped, another town that needed an agency or office. Ending up in Fallen Tree Gulch, which most people had shortened to Fallwood, on the Nebraska–Colorado border, for the night, was not intentional, only a result of not wanting to travel any farther that day. As it had been too early to turn in, he chose to sit in at a two-bit-ante card game.

Tito discovered the other three men at the table to be a store clerk, a nearby rancher, and one of his new hired hands, a young, rather stoutly built cowboy named Darby. The talk was light and easy, the pots relatively small, and the four were nearly even after a full hour of play. That was when a new man approached the table. Tito had noticed him earlier, loud, belligerent, with the cocky swagger of a man who thought a great deal of himself. Without an invite, he pulled out a chair and plopped down. The two older men displayed annoyance, but neither voiced an objection.

"You fellows look like sheep to be fleeced," the new arrival said and snorted.

The newcomer was six feet tall, with shaggy,

mustard-colored hair, pale green eyes, and a bulb nose over thick, wide lips. Tito didn't fancy the looks of him. He could also smell the whiskey on the man's breath. His better judgment told him that he ought to pick up his money and call it quits. However, he had never been able to back away from a bully, so he stayed.

"Ain't seen you around these parts before, kid," the man said to the young cowboy.

"Name's Darby."

"Yeah? Where do you work?"

"He's a new man I hired on," the rancher replied.

"And how 'bout you, Spanish?" he said, observing Tito's frock jacket, open to expose an expensive black vest, decorated with several conchos. He locked gazes, begrudgingly admiring the wide silver band on Tito's black hat. "I don't recognize you neither."

"Tito Pacheco," he answered, "and I'm not working for anyone around here."

"Me, I'm Saul Puggot," he boasted, as if the name ought to mean something.

"Two-bit ante, Puggot," Tito told him.

"Kids' game," he said and snickered. "What say we make this game more interesting? How about a dollar ante and no limit on the bets?"

The store clerk slid back his chair. "Too rich for my blood."

Saul scalded him with a narrow gaze. "Sit down, Zack. You make a fortune in that store of yours. You can stand to lose a few coins."

The man hesitated, then moved back up to the table. "Maybe a hand or two, but I can't stay late."

"I expect it's my deal," Saul announced with a crooked grin. "New man always gets the deal."

Tito prided himself on being a slow man to rile, so he put up with the man's obnoxious manners. It had actually been his turn with the deck, but the cards hadn't been doing him any favors. He decided that a change of dealers might be good for his luck.

Saul bought thirty dollars' worth of chips and flipped out the ante. Then he shuffled the cards with a smooth, effortless motion. Tito observed that this was a man who handled pasteboards on a regular basis. He had quick fingers and a number of flashy moves.

Accepted as a traveler or drummer, rather than a gambler, Tito could sit in on games that might otherwise have been closed to a man of his skill. He wasn't a polished professional, but he had learned a good many tricks of the trade. During his youth, he had spent a lot of time with his uncle, who had been a professional gambling man down in Mexico City. Silver Stud Pacheco, most people had called him, a fair hand at nearly every form of gambling. He had been a flamboyant dresser, a smooth talker, with a quick smile and quicker hands. He still lived in Mexico, but Tito had been forced to leave his home country after the French had been driven out. He had not been back to see him since. Still he remembered a good many of the lessons the man had taught him. Silver had told him he was a natural, but gambling had never seemed much of a life for Tito, only a way to pass some time. He smiled inwardly, recalling how the game had been Silver's whole life. He had bragged to Tito that, if gambling was banned in heaven, he'd take out a deck of cards and play the Devil for his soul.

"Your bet, Slick," Saul prompted Darby. It caused Tito to return his attention to the game.

The youth glanced at his cards. "Open for two bits."

Saul snickered. "Got me some high rollers here tonight; I shore do."

The night progressed and Tito held his own. Saul was no slouch at draw poker, but he was like a good many gamblers, not simply trusting to his skill and luck. He took advantage of the other three men at the table, palming a card now and again, or slipping one from the bottom of the deck. Tito saw him use the extra card trick and let it go. Even with a sixth card, Saul didn't have a bidding hand. But a couple rounds later, with Saul dealing once more, Tito spied an ace on the bottom of the deck. When Saul raised the pot, the card was no longer there!

"It's to you, Slick." Saul nudged the young cowboy. "You in or out?"

Tito glanced at the other men. They were all down a considerable amount. The cowboy was sweating, having watched his first month's wages disappear since Puggot sat down.

"Fold," he said, pitching his cards onto the table.

Saul reached for the pot, but Tito spoke up. "I'm in," he said, "and raise twenty."

That got everyone's attention. "Twenty?" Saul did not hide his surprise.

"Twenty," Tito repeated, tossing in two of the ten-dollar chips.

The man shook his head and set his teeth. "You

ain't got the high hand this time, Spanish. I'm cleaning house.''

''You'll need twenty more to prove it,'' Tito repeated.

Saul fingered his cards and frowned. He had the extra ace he'd dealt from the bottom, but Tito had tossed an ace to fill his own hand. That meant Saul could be holding three aces, perhaps even a full house. But it wasn't good enough. This time, his cheating was not going to help.

''All right, Spanish,'' he said, tossing the chips into the middle, ''I'm calling you. What are you so proud of?''

''Pretty red hearts, five through nine, a straight flush,'' Tito said, spreading them out on the table. ''Even with the ace of spades you dealt yourself off the bottom of the deck, you're beat.''

Saul's face worked. He glared at the cards, then up at Tito with hate-filled eyes. ''What are you saying, that I don't play straight, Spanish?''

Tito offered a mirthless smile as he rested his right hand on the butt of his Colt Peacemaker. ''Not at all, Puggot. I was only making an observation.''

''You've been dealing off the bottom!'' Darby snarled. Enraged, he jumped to his feet. ''You stole my money, you rotten cheat!'' He raised his fists. ''I'm going to use your face for a broom!''

''Wait, Darby!'' the rancher tried to calm him. ''Don't—''

But Saul pushed back from the table, knocking over his chair. ''Nobody calls Saul Puggot a cheat!'' he said with a snarl, making a grab for his pistol.

Darby had been ready to fight, but he wasn't even

wearing a gun. The instant he realized that Puggot was drawing on him, his eyes bugged with alarm and he threw out his hands, as if to ward off the bullets. Puggot could not miss him at point-blank range.

Tito did the only thing he could to save the young man. He jerked free his own gun and fired—a split-second before Puggot could pull the trigger. It knocked the man back a step. He sagged forward, the pistol slipped from his fingers, and he spilled, face-down, onto the table. Chips and drinks were knocked onto the floor by his collapsing body. The room was suddenly quiet enough to have heard a gnat sneeze.

Darby's bloodless face was twisted into a mask of shock. He slowly lowered his hands and rotated around to stare at Tito.

"He'd have kilt me certain," he barely whispered.

Tito got to his feet and holstered his gun. He knew Puggot was dead. Few men were quicker to get a gun into play than he, and fewer still were any better at placing the shot. He'd targeted the left side of Puggot's vest pocket and drilled the slug right through his heart. All he had wanted was a quiet evening, some friendly conversation over a game of cards. Now a man was dead.

"You did what you had to, Pacheco," the rancher said solemnly. "I'm thanking you for the lad's life."

The store owner was grim. "It's too durn bad this had to happen. When word reaches Baxter Puggot, Saul's brother, neither of you are going to be able to find a hole deep enough that he won't root you out. He'll hunt you down and kill you both for sure."

"What are you talking about?" Darby was incredulous. "Hey! I didn't even have a gun!"

"The circumstances won't matter to Baxter Puggot. You boys would be smart to cut for the sand and sage and not look back."

The rancher handed Darby some folded paper money. "Sorry about this, son. Zack's right. There ain't no law this side of the North Platte. You men best leave town and not look back. When Baxter arrives to reckon for Saul's death, he'll shoot first and won't have no questions later. Saul was a bully, a liar, and a cheat, but it don't change the fact he was Baxter Puggot's brother. That's the only thing that will matter."

Darby's jaw worked and he set his teeth together. "Maybe me and Pacheco here ain't of a mind to run. We maybe ought to stick around and settle with Baxter. I ain't no coward."

"Bravery has nothing to do with it, son. Baxter has a half-dozen hard and ruthless men who ride for him. They're a bunch of bounty hunters, mean and ruthless killers, every single one. They even work for the Army on occasion, rounding up renegade Indians. They've brought in bandits from Kansas, Colorado, Nebraska, and even Wyoming. They have contacts for a hundred miles in any direction and spend most of their time chasing down any man with a price on his head."

The storekeeper's head bobbed up and down in agreement. "Worse than that, boys, far as I know, they have never brung back a man alive. Everyone in Fallwood has been forced to put up with Saul's tough-guy act, because no one wanted to cross Baxter."

"Didn't even have time to unpack my gear," Darby said dejectedly.

"I was going to leave in the morning anyway," Tito

said, suffering the discomfort of a flood of acid attacking his stomach. He wondered how the Wells Fargo brass would react to his killing a man over a stupid game of cards. Worse, now he was on the run from a pack of hard-case gunmen.

Chapter Two

Juanita Lopez paused to wipe her brow with the back of her hand. She was glad to be nearly finished with the laundry. Once she heat-pressed the last shirt with the heavy iron, she would be finished for the night.

Pablo, her brother, entered the house. He had a worried frown showing on his face. Juanita placed the iron on the stove hot plate so it would reheat. She didn't have to ask what was troubling Pablo, for he had the milk bucket in his hand. He reluctantly tipped it so she could see the bottom.

"Not enough milk to satisfy a kitten's appetite, Sis. What are we going to do about Inez?"

Juanita automatically glanced over at the cradle. The baby was sleeping soundly at the moment, but she would be hungry very soon. "We'll mix some warm water with it. Maybe Daisy will give a little more milk in the morning."

"I wouldn't count on it. She's been trying to dry up for the past two months. Can't expect a milk cow to produce year after year without stopping to have a calf."

"The money is due for this laundry tomorrow. It ought to buy us a few tins of condensed milk and something for the table."

"Winter is only a month or two away. How long can we get by until we all starve, Sis?" The concern in Pablo's voice was distinct. "Papa should have been back days ago. What if he never comes back?"

"He wouldn't desert us."

"I'm not saying he would, but what if he was way-laid by some Indians or dry-gulched by bandits on the trail? What if someone seen him packing all that money around?"

Papa wouldn't have advertised that he was carrying so much money. He was going to look for us a place, before he cashed the voucher. Maybe he found a farm or something and had to wait for a few days to talk to the owner or something."

"You really think Papa was serious about finding us a new home? I mean, what kind of a farm could he buy with the sixty dollars we earned working the fields?"

"You know how he is," Juanita answered. "He hated the work of harvesting field after field of beans. I'm sure he's been looking for something else, a place where we can start our own crops."

Pablo let the subject drop as he carefully poured the trickle of milk into a jar. Even with adding some water, there was barely enough for a single feeding for the baby. He sighed at the meager amount and walked over to look down at the youngest member of the Lopez family. A compassionate look flooded his features. "She has the same large brown eyes as Mama," he said softly. "I'll bet she's the pick of the litter." He cocked his head around to face Juanita. "Not that you aren't right easy on the eyes too!"

Juanita tried to smile, but it was hard to concern

herself with her appearance when she was dead tired from endless chores. The eldest of seven children, she was weary of trying to raise and feed herself and six siblings. Pablo was two years behind her own eighteen, Ricky, at fourteen, did a lot to help, and Ruban, twelve, was eager to lend a hand, but the bulk of the load still rested on her shoulders.

"Tend to the fire, Pablo. I'll be ready to start supper pretty soon."

"Did Ruban and Ricky get any game?"

"One cottontail."

"That's something, but one rabbit won't go very far."

"I needed the boys to watch Gena, Maria, and the baby. They didn't have a lot of time. We only have to make do until Papa gets back. Then we'll have us a real feast. You can eat till you bust."

"I think I'll dream about that tonight."

Juanita watched him leave with the bucket. She was glad her brother was strong and supportive. He never complained about the work and duties that were piled on him. It had often fell to him to be the man of the house, even when their father was at home. Hermando Lopez was a dreamer and a nomad. He talked of the big house they would have one day, vowed there would be a garden, chickens, and separate rooms for the girls and the boys. But his words were empty promises, the same as he had given her mother for almost twenty years.

For a moment, she stared out the shanty's one window, wishing with all her might to see Hermando coming. Why was it taking him so long to return with the money they had earned working in the fields? He had never been very reliable, but he would not have deserted his family.

She felt the pressure of the world on her diminutive shoulders. There were hungry children to feed, she had the baby to worry about, and they couldn't stay in the dilapidated shack forever. It was about to fall down around their ears, full of splinters and decayed from years of neglect. The wooden slabs were cracked and weathered until it barely kept out the wind, and the roof leaked in more places than not. If they had to spend a winter there, they would all freeze to death.

Blinking at the tears that tried to surface in her eyes, she stared at the dirt floor. She had swept it over and over until it was a hard-pack surface, but her bare feet were still blacked from the fine dust. Dressed in rags, living like a pack of coyotes, viewed by their neighbors as vagrants and beggars, it was a horrid existence.

Juanita firmed her resolve once more and took up the towel she used to protect her hand from the heat of the iron's handle. She removed the heavy, hot iron from the stove and began to smooth the wrinkles from the material on the table. She silently cursed herself for giving in to depression while she worked to make the shirt as perfect as possible. If she could impress the judge, he might let her do his laundry again. With luck, he might tell a few others and she would get enough work to keep the household going.

Her mind thought back to before her mother had died during childbirth with Inez. There had been little difference in her life. She had always been the one responsible for the children. Her mother had been frail and sickly for several years. The pregnancy had been the ultimate physical hardship for her, resulting in her death.

Juanita accepted the duties without complaint. She saw to the needs of the children as best she could. They shared a washtub for a monthly bath, she cut the boys' hair and did the laundry, cooking, and house cleaning. With a little help from Gena, who was ten, she also tended six-year-old Maria and the baby. It left her jaded and red-eyed from lack of sleep, but there was no one else to do the work. Worse, if Hermando didn't show up pretty soon, she and Pablo would have to find real jobs that paid wages.

Keeping a roof over their heads was one more concern to worry about. At their arrival in Ivory Flats, Everett Toller had let them move into the shanty on the condition they help with his chores several days a week. Hermando hadn't done a day's work since they finished harvesting the last of the beans. That meant Everett was doing the chores alone. He was bound to grow impatient and demand they vacate the shack. There were a good many families around trying to make a living by sharecropping or working for the few successful farmers or ranchers in the area. If the Lopez family didn't live up to their end of the bargain, he could demand they move out. Juanita experienced a queasy feeling at the thought. What would she do, if they ended up without shelter?

Father will be back soon, she told herself. There was a logical reason for his delay in returning. All she needed to do was hang on for a little while longer.

Darby knelt down to look over the body. Tito sat his palomino and held the young man's horse, assailed by the stench of death, uneasy at being so near the remains of a man and what was left of his horse. It amazed him that Darby could poke and prod a man who had been dead for hours or possibly even days.

"Busted leg," Darby announced. "Bled quite a bit from where the bone broke through the skin. Probably died from shock and loss of blood."

"Shock?"

"That's a medical term I learnt from my pa. He was a medico during the big war. I used to listen to his stories for hours on end. Tell you what, Pacheco, I plum lost my cookies a time or two."

"Sure can't tell you have a weak stomach by the way you're able to examine that corpse."

"Funny, ain't it?" he replied. "Maybe I should take me a job as a mortician. Seems that a dead body don't bother me none."

"I'd guess the guy's horse fell and they both ended up with broken legs. He was riding so far off the main trail that no one came by to help. What do you think?"

"I'd say you're on the money, Pacheco." He gave the body another once-over. "I make him to be Mexican, at least forty years old, slender build, with a streak of gray running through his hair. He's wearing cheap work shoes, ragged clothes and,"—he searched the man's coat and trousers—"has a watch, seven cents, and a faded receipt in his pocket." He examined the paper. "Looks like a voucher of some kind."

"Can you read a name?"

"Nope." Then Darby picked up the man's pistol and checked it. "He fired all of his ammo, probably trying to summon help. If we hadn't been going cross-country to reach the main trail toward Denver, we wouldn't have found him. Bet he was taking a shortcut too.''

Tito pointed at several mounds of dirt a few yards from where the horse lay. "There's the culprits, a city of prairie dogs. Horse might have been moving too fast and broke a leg.''

"Either that, or he was traveling in the dark.''

"Probably one or the other.''

"So what do we do with the body?''

"Two choices," Tito answered. "We can either bury him or make a travois and drag his body to Helpful. That's the closest town.''

"The old boy isn't a pretty sight to be dragging down the main street of town, Pacheco. My vote is to plant him right here and report his demise to the local sheriff.''

Tito neck-reined his horse over to a nearby bush. "I'll get started on the hole, if you want to use the fellow's blanket to wrap him up.''

An hour later, the body was lowered into a rectangular hole. Darby stepped back and stood with his hat in his hand, waiting for Tito to say the words over the body.

"Lord, we didn't know this stranger, but I imagine You did. If You allow that he earned it, take his soul.'' He thought for a moment, but decided he'd about covered everything. "Amen.''

"It's plain to see that you ain't the long-winded sort to ever take up preaching gospel, Pacheco. Mayhaps I'll take up pen and paper and set down my own final words, in case I meet my own demise while riding with you.''

"Can't plead a fellow's case, if I didn't at least know him."

"Well, for his sake, let's hope he wasn't a border-line sort, who needed a little extra push to get into heaven."

A few minutes later, the dirt and sand had covered the body and they each stood before the mound in a final moment of silence. Tito shoved his hat onto his head. "Time's a-wasting, Darby. We'll need to kick up some dust to make Helpful before dark."

"I won't be holding us back," he said quickly. "Let's move."

Chapter Three

The two Indians had run their horses to ground, then continued on foot until they both gave out too. They were armed only with an old musket and a hunting knife between them. When Baxter Puggot and his boys caught up with them, they threw their hands up to surrender.

Baxter covered them with his gun while Quint and Trapper searched them for weapons. Nolen, Marx, and Walt were also present. They sat back and waited, watching the action without displaying any emotion.

"Be a lot of trouble watching these two characters," Walt finally spoke up. "If they was to get loose during the night or something, they'd sure enough cut our throats."

Baxter didn't even flinch. He pulled the trigger on his gun—twice, three times! And the two Indians fell to the ground, both mortally wounded.

"That suit you, Walt?"

Walt laughed. "You do know the short way to make our job easier, Bax."

Nolen stepped forward to check the bodies. "This one ain't more'n a boy, maybe sixteen or so."

"They stole horses and were armed," Quint said.

"I'd say they were going to cause a lot more trouble before they were finished."

But Nolen only shook his head. "No more'n boys," he said again.

"Good thing it's only a day's ride to the fort," Trapper said to change the subject. "Hauling dead bodies in this heat can become unpleasant real sudden."

"Yonder is a rider coming," Walt said, gazing past the men on horseback. "Looks like Chiggers."

Marx had the best eyes in the group. He swung about in his saddle. "Yep, it's Chiggers all right. Wonder why he's tracking us?"

"Maybe another job," Quint suggested.

Baxter reined his horse around, walking it toward the approaching rider. Chiggers often rode with them, but the day they left, he had been sick from too much drink and unable to get out of bed. Baxter figured Quint was probably right about more work. There were always cattle or horse thefts, claim jumpers, or someone on the dodge from the law in nearby states or territories. As professional manhunters for hire, they were a carefree group who lived for the enjoyment of the chase and bounty on their prey.

Chiggers rode the horse at a full gallop, right up until he reached Baxter. Then he pulled back the reins to stop the animal. His mount was blowing hard from the long run. Chiggers himself was out of breath from the strenuous effort.

"I ought to scald your hide, Chiggers!" Baxter snarled, taking note of the lather on his horse. "You forget how to treat a horse? I done told you a hundred times that your steed is more important out here than reading sign!''

"Yeah, I know, Bax, but this couldn't wait until you come back to town.''

"What's happened?''

"Your brother," Chiggers blurted, ''he's been killed!''

The bluntness of the information stunned Baxter. He was unable to speak, struck with a sudden rush of anguish and regret that completely overwhelmed him.

"Saul?'' he choked out the name.

"Yeah, it was over a game of cards.'' He went on to relate sketchy details about the gunfight.

Baxter overcame his grief to gnash his teeth. "The stupid moron!'' He cursed vehemently. "What was Saul doing getting into a gunfight? He couldn't hit the side of a saloon, if he was pulling the trigger from the inside!''

"I'm right sorry, Bax.''

"What about the two cowpokes who gunned him down?''

"They left town.''

"I'll bet they did.'' Baxter growled the words. "Which way?''

"No one knows for certain. The one was a new cowpoke in town, and the other was a well-dressed Mexican, who was riding a fine-looking palomino. We shouldn't have a lot of trouble tracking them down.''

The leader of the band sat his mount in contemplation for a few seconds. He finally returned to the present and looked over his men. "We need to take those two renegades to the fort and collect the money due us. Then we'll spread out and see where the Mexican and that there cowboy ran off to. Ain't no one going to get away with killing my brother. If I have to chase them from now till cows crow and chickens bay at the moon, I'll run them to ground.''

"Whatever you say, Bax. You only got to say what you want me to do.''

"You return with us, Chiggers, after you rub down your horse and give it a rest. Nolen is our packer. He and Trapper can ride ahead. Nolen can get our supplies ready while Trapper sends out some wires to a few of our nearby contacts. With some luck, we might get a line on those two murdering sons by the time we are ready to light out after them.''

From a few feet away, Marx grinned at Quint. "Strange man, our leader. He'll put a bullet into an Indian or thief to watch 'im die, but he'll bust your head for mistreating a horse.''

"Hear what Chiggers said?'' Quint replied in a hushed reply. "Someone killed Saul.''

"Only thing amazes me is why it took so long. Saul was about as worthless as a fishnet rain slicker.''

"Ain't that the dying truth?'' Quint agreed. "You can be sure it won't stop Bax from doing what he says. We're going to see the men dead who are responsible.''

"Yup, sounds as if we've got some new tracking to do.''

"Think Bax would get riled if we were to shake those fellows' hands before we killed them?''

"We maybe should keep it to ourselves,'' Marx advised. "Bax ain't going to be in a mood for any levity connected to his brother for a spell.''

"I guess we best lend a hand loading up the bodies

of those two Indians. I suspect we're not going to spend the night.''

The nearest thing to a town marshal in Helpful was a shop owner and gunsmith named Clovis Joy. He sported a shock of red hair and a complexion that looked lie a freckle farm. When Tito and Darby entered his leather store, he greeted them with a wide smile, displaying a gap between his front teeth.

''Howdy, boys!'' he offered. Then, with a quick once-over, he said, ''Bet I know from whence you two fellows came.''

Tito caught Darby's worried look. ''That so?'' he asked.

''Only one place around here where you can pick up that red dust, over at Rusty Hills, about twenty miles due north.''

''You got us figured right,'' Tito admitted, noting Darby's sigh of relief.

''Let's see,'' Clovis appraised them shortly, pausing to study Tito's expensive clothes and lastly looked at his hands. ''You are a native of the West, possibly a gambler or drummer of sorts. You don't do a lot of physical work, except for the callus on your thumb— proof that you spend time working with the gun on your hip.''

Tito reached up to tip back his hat. He wondered what kind of character they had run up against.

''Your friend here appears to be a cowboy.'' With another moment of study, Clovis said, ''But still new at the trade.''

''How can you tell that?'' Darby wanted to know.

''The inside of your boots don't have the wear from

the stirrups rubbing when you bust a bronc, and your hands don't show the hardness of a man who works with a rope. Besides that, you don't have the leather skin of a man who spends sixteen hours a day in a saddle.''

"You a Pinkerton man or something?"

He laughed. ''No, but I've been reading the *Police Gazette* since before the war. Them detective fellers are sharp as needlepoints.''

Tito turned to Darby. ''Appears we've found the right man for the job at hand. If anyone can sort out the dead man we come across, it'll be Clovis here.''

"Dead man, you say?"

''At the entrance to those Rusty Hills you mentioned, maybe twenty-five miles back. The old boy run his horse into a city of prairie dogs. Ended up with a busted leg and a dead horse. From what we could tell, he died yesterday or last night.

''Man looked to be Mexican, in his late forties, brown hair, with a streak of white on the top of his head. He was dressed poor, with nothing but an oil slicker and blanket on his horse. Only thing we found, he had this on him.'' Tito dug out the paper from his shirt pocket. ''Plus seven cents, and a Dennison-Howard watch. It don't work.''

Clovis turned the paper around, held it up to the light, and then spread it out on the counter. ''Good quality paper, but the writing is faded and smeared. The guy probably got it wet.''

"We couldn't get a word out of it."

After a moment, Clovis picked up a small cleaning brush and dipped a bit of water out of a nearby bucket. He added one drop of ink to the water and then carefully wet the brush and ran it across the page, wetting it with the tip.

"Sometimes, if the writer pressed hard enough with the pencil, you can get an imprint," he explained. Then he used a magnifying glass and studied the page for a few seconds. "Ivory Flats," he said. "The fellow's name is too blurred to make out, but the town is Ivory Flats, about sixty miles from the Kansas border."

"I rode through there one time," Tito said. "Seems there were a good many farms over that way."

"The guy's name looks to begin with an *H*, but it's too faint to read. Whoever wrote this out, they didn't use a decent grade of ink, and they didn't press down very hard." He glanced up. "Any idea what this piece of paper is?"

"I've seen a few of them around," Tito replied. "It's the part of a pay voucher that is used as a receipt by Wells Fargo. When you present the voucher, the agent at Wells Fargo hands you your money and takes the voucher. This is the copy they give the customer for the completed transaction."

"You seem to know something of Wells Fargo."

"I should. I work for them."

"Any ideas?"

"I'd say that there must not be a bank in Ivory Flats. The gent we found probably made a trip and cashed the voucher."

"But he only had the seven cents on him?"

"That's right, and we didn't see any other tracks around. If he was robbed of any money, it would have been before we arrived."

"Unless he hid or buried it after he ended up stranded with a busted leg," Darby said.

"We didn't dig anything but a grave," Tito told Clovis. "It didn't seem important at the time."

"Like as not, if the guy was still dressed in rags, he lost the money or had already used it up. Can't make out the amount or date, and this voucher is too worn to pick out any identifying number for tracing the receipt."

"Got to be a bank or Wells Fargo office between here and Ivory Flats," Darby said, thinking aloud. "Why do you think he made the longer trip?"

"Might have wanted to buy something special or look over the lay of the land," Clovis suggested. "With the Utes being moved onto reservations, there is more land for settling to the west. Of course, you are only guessing which way he was headed. What if he was going the opposite direction?"

"From the way the horse fell, I'm pretty certain he was coming this way."

"Could have been heading back to Ivory Flats," Clovis suggested. "From where you say you found him, it would be a straight shot from there."

"Sounds possible, all right."

"So, what's your plan, fellows?"

"Our plan?"

"Well, you boys found the body," Clovis said. "I think you ought to take a ride over to Ivory Flats and see if you can locate anyone who knows the dead man. It would be a good deed."

"That's an expensive good deed," Darby said. "A full day's ride in the saddle to get there, then maybe not even find anyone who knew him."

"You said he had a distinguishing mark, the white streak in his hair, and either his first or last name begins with an *H*. What could be simpler?"

Tito sighed. "I guess someone ought to make the trip. Might as well be me."

"I'll tag along," Darby added. "Like the man here says, we were the ones who found the body."

Baxter stood at the grave, hat in his hands. His head was bowed, partly out of grief, but mostly so no one would be able to see the tears in his eyes.

"You big dumb kid," he murmured under his breath. "Why did you make a play for your gun? The cowboy was unarmed. You should have taken him on with your fists! I swear, you never did have a brain in your head."

"We're ready, Bax," Nolen said from a few feet behind him.

Baxter cleared his throat and blinked away the last of the tears. He shoved his hat onto his head and turned to look over his men.

"I figure to head south with Quint," Nolen outlined, "till we hit the main fork. Then Quint will continue toward Kansas and I'll head Colorado way. We'll check every town for a hundred miles, until we get a lead on those two. Trapper is going to ride north with you. Marx and Walt will go east and Chiggers is going west."

"Not much chance they went west," Baxter said, noticing the big man was not in the group.

"Why do you think we decided to send Chiggers that way?" Nolen offered a slight grin. "Good man in a fight, but he couldn't track an elephant going through a cornfield.''

"I don't expect the boys to work for nothing, Nolen. I want these two hombres, and I'll pay the price. I'm putting up five hundred in gold for their heads, out of my own pocket.''

Trapper came forward to join them. He gave a negative shake of his head. "No one is going to put a Wanted poster out on them, Bax. If we catch them, we have to force them into a fight.''

"Trapper's right,'' Nolen agreed. "The killing was a fair fight. According to the barkeep, he said how several men witnessed the shooting. Your brother drew down on the one called Darby, but the fellow didn't have a gun. The Mexican shot Saul before he could kill an unarmed man.''

Baxter regarded Nolen with hateful eyes. "Then buzzards kilt my brother! I don't care if he was about to kill a priest! No one gets away with murdering my kid brother!''

"I was only making a point, Bax.''

"If you ain't got the stomach for this, you can stay behind.''

Trapper waved a hand, as if to dismiss any question. "We're with you on this all the way, Bax. You know you can count on us.''

Nolen didn't respond to his harsh words. He knew how much Baxter loved Saul. The kid was about as worthless as a second belly button, but he had been Baxter's brother. That's all that counted.

Baxter eased up on his two men. He needed to keep them happy. If he was to do all of the looking by himself, he might never get a line on the two men who killed his brother. He gave a short nod, as if to dismiss any concern, then started off in the direction of their horses. "Let's get moving."

Chapter Four

It was called Ivory Flats, because there wasn't a hill in sight and Ivory was the name of the first man who settled the area. It was a tough little burg that had fought long and hard to survive. The War Between the States had bankrupted the town, then much of it had been burned to the ground during the Indian wars. However, it was on the road to recovery now. It had been a good year for crops and there was a constant influx of tenant workers or hopeful farmers searching for land. Along with the growth and prosperity, there were new problems from the change. Some of the longtime farmers resented the newcomers. Others hired the impoverished black or white families for pennies, treating them no better than slave labor. They would often supply food or housing, then deduct so many expenses that the workers or sharecroppers ended up working for free. Added to the dilemma, there were more farmers looking for home sites than there was room. The overcrowding caused jealousy and fights among the newcomers and the established tenant farmers.

As Tito and Darby entered town, they saw a gathering of people. There came some shouting and jeering, the kind that Tito had seen a number of times before.

"Got a fight going," he told Darby.

"Let's have a look."

They drew closer, and from the vantage point of being on horseback, they could see a young Mexican, still in his teens, was mixing it up with another man, perhaps ten years older. The difference in experience was evident at first glance.

The younger man took wild swings and got mostly air. The other fellow blocked or ducked his attack and then smacked the kid full in the face. He nailed him good and solid with a couple follow-up shots, knocking him to the ground.

"Get up, squatter!" He spat out the words. "I've got plenty more to give you!"

"Stop it!" A young senorita shouted, pushing her way through the crowd. She rushed over to the beaten youth and threw herself over his body. "You've knocked him senseless!" she cried. "Isn't that enough?"

"Stinkin' squatters!" a voice boomed from the crowd. "Ought to run them all out of the country!"

Another joined in the taunting. "Stomp him into the ground, Reel. Make him into fertilizer!"

The man called Reel went after the boy again. He roughly shoved the girl away and grabbed the young man by the shirt, ready to drag him up onto his feet.

"I'd say the boy's had enough," Tito found himself speaking up over the jeers of the crowd. It brought forth a hush and all eyes turned toward him.

The man called Reel let go of the kid and stared at

Tito with a curious gaze. "What's it to you, stranger?"

"Nothing at all, friend," Tito replied easily. "I was simply making an observation."

The crowd parted between the man and Tito. He wore a black vest, flat-crowned white hat, polished boots, and denim pants. The sneer on his lips was that of a confident man. He turned his head and spat a stream of tobacco juice into the dust. His eyes glistened with anticipation as he put his attention back on Tito.

"Sounds to me like you're taking sides with this shiftless bum."

"Not me." Tito kept his voice cool and tranquil. "I was only speaking up for a hapless fellow who isn't able to speak for himself."

"Maybe you'd like to join him?"

Tito glanced at the semiconscious form. "It appears to me he's bleeding just fine all by himself."

The twist of humor caused the man to lower his guard. "You're right about that much, stranger. What's your name?"

"Tito Pacheco."

He glanced at Darby but didn't ask for his name. Instead, he pulled back his vest to reveal a tin badge pinned to his shirt. "Me, I'm Vince Reel, deputy sheriff of Ivory Flats."

That bit of news came as a surprise. Tito displayed a friendly grin. "Tough town you've got, Deputy. Is the punishment for vagrancy being beaten into a heap?"

"Vagrancy?" Reel didn't recognize the word.

"Being a person with no home and no money."

"Oh, yeah," he agreed, then eyed Tito a bit closer. "You two don't look all that much different than the kid here. You a couple saddle tramps or what?"

"I'd say we're in the *or what* category, Deputy. I'm taking some time off from my employment and the fellow with me is between jobs."

Reel cast a final look at the beaten young man and walked over to stand a few feet from Darby and Tito. He surveyed them once more and spat again. The act was to look tough, but he didn't manage the feat without dribbling down his chin. He quickly wiped it with the back of his hand, but the pretense of being an accomplished tobacco spitter was lost.

"Not much work in these parts, boys. Especially for men who like to do their work from the back of a horse."

"I've not seen much but farms for the past fifty miles, that's a fact."

"What else can I do for you?"

"We've about worn our horse's hooves off to their knees from riding the past couple days. Maybe you can tell us where we can put up for a little recuperation and something to eat." He displayed a mirthless smile. "Some place neutral?"

Reel chuckled. "You won't find no such place as neutral in Ivory, Pacheco. Either you back the established farmers and sharecroppers, or you back the newcomers and squatters."

"We aren't of a mind to join either side of a dispute, Deputy. Perhaps we can rest the horses for a day or so and then ride on."

"Good thinking," he said. Then he rotated about to look at the gawking crowd of people. "Well?" he asked them as a group. "Get on with your business! There ain't no show going on now!"

The people broke up into smaller groups or shuffled off. The battered young man was sitting up under his own power, being attended by the girl, who had come to his aid. Tito didn't offer a closer look, not wanting to incur the wrath of the deputy.

"Yonder is the livery," Reel said, tipping his head in that direction. "You'll find a rooming house up the street that might fit you in for a night or two."

"Much obliged," Tito said, and watched as the deputy walked away. Once out of earshot, he turned to Darby. "Let's put up the horses and get something to eat. We'll check around when things die down a little."

"Thought we was in it there, Pard. You see how that deputy kept his right hand on his gun? You're lucky he didn't draw down on us."

"Think so?"

"I'm beginning to think you're lucky at more than cards. He might have up and killed us both."

"The man never removed the thong from the hammer on his gun," Tito informed him matter-of-factly. "Most of our deputy's talk was a tough act for the sake of the people watching."

Darby's head jerked around and he checked Tito's own gun. The leather strap was not in place. "Is that luck too? You'd have had him under your Colt before he had a chance to draw his own pistol."

"Not luck exactly, more like being prepared."

"Let's see if your luck holds up for a good meal. I'm starved."

* * *

Back at their shanty, Pablo held the wet cloth to his face. The bleeding had stopped, but his left eye was swollen shut and his lower lip was about twice its normal size. Juanita sat plaintively at his side, her mind working as she tried to formulate a logical plan of action. The cupboards were empty, Ruben and Ricky had not found any game, and the baby was starting to fuss for something to fill her tummy.

"Sorry, Sis," Pablo said quietly, "I shouldn't have started yelling at the owner of the trading post."

"It's not your fault. We were cheated on the price of those furs. I know Mr. Authen gives a better price to other people, at least, the ones who own property."

"Yeah, but we're squatters!" He sighed. "And now that the crops are done, we don't even have work anymore. Unless Mr. Toller decides to hire us on through the winter, we're going to be considered no better than vultures."

"Our immediate concern is for Inez and the children. We've got to eat."

"You have all of our money, big sister." He attempted a grin, but the swollen lip made it more of a grimace. "At least you were smart enough to pick up the coins Authen tossed onto the counter, before Vince showed up."

"Yes, and I have what the judge paid me, but we still have only a little over a dollar! How long can we live on that?"

"I think we ought to butcher Daisy. She's gone bone dry, and she's too along in years to have another calf. You know that's the reason the guy gave her to us; they were moving to Colorado and she couldn't keep up with their wagon."

Juanita felt the weight of defeat. "Other than Papa's horse, she's the only animal we own. If we did butcher her, then what? We'd have nothing!"

"Papa isn't here to make the decision, but it's what he would do if he were here."

"I suppose, but . . ."

"You've been saying it for the last two weeks, we only have to get by until he returns. Once he gets back, everything will be all right. Our job is to get by until he does."

"I wish I was as certain as you. Papa hasn't been the same since Mama died. I wonder sometimes if he will ever come back."

"He wouldn't desert us."

Juanita forced a tight smile. "Of course he wouldn't."

"We have to do what is necessary and hold on a little longer."

"We won't be able to do that if you start fighting with men like Vince Reel. He's twice your size. I thought he was going to kill you with his bare hands!"

Pablo grunted his agreement. "He hits a lot harder than I thought he could too. You won't need to remind me to not go up against him again."

"Good thing that stranger butted in," she said. "I don't know if it's because he was a Mexican like us, or if he felt sorry for your pitiful condition."

"Pitiful?"

"Yes, pitiful."

"Vince knocked me down, but I was holding my own."

"Your eyes were rolling around like a couple marbles on a china plate. The only thing you were doing on your own was bleeding.''

"Oh," Pablo said, ducking his head, "*that* kind of pitiful."

"That man saved what's left of your hide. Vince had up a head of steam. He was going to pound on you some more."

"I might not have put up a great fight, but I did hit him pretty good that first punch." He chuckled at the memory. "Only punch I landed."

"If by some miracle you had whipped him, then what? You can't fight against the law and win."

"Vince is a rowdy blowhard. He doesn't represent the law in Ivory Flats."

"It wouldn't matter much, if you ended up in jail!"

Pablo didn't argue. "You better go ahead and make the trip to the store, big sister. I'll just sit here and soak my head and feel sorry for myself."

Juanita counted the change. "A measly dollar and three cents won't go far."

"Ruban and Ricky can go hunting again tomorrow. Maybe they'll get us something. If not"—he lifted his shoulders in a shrug—"it might be time to butcher our cow. We could trade a little of the meat for eggs and flour."

"Then what do we do, Pablo? We are facing winter in a few weeks. Even if there were jobs—and there aren't any—no one is going to hire people our age. There are mature men with families who can't even find work."

"What do you think we should do?"

Juanita's dark brows knitted in thought. "What we need is a grown man to help. If we had a man in the family, we might find a place of our own doing share-cropping. Papa said he had a few places lined up, before we took on the bean harvest.''

"He took the fieldwork so we could all pitch in. Papa has never been the most ambitious sort.''

Juanita didn't like to malign their father, but she had grown weary of bumming around from one place to the next. In her entire life, they had never spent two winters under the same roof. Eighteen years of moving, taking odd jobs, dealing for meals or begging for a little work. It was not a pleasant way to live.

"If Papa doesn't show up in the next day or two, I'll speak to Mr. Toller. He might be willing to let us stay here and do chores for him. Between you, me, and Ricky, we can do quite a bit of work. If not, it would only take a little bit of money to get our own place somewhere.''

"And be squatters!''

"No!'' she was emphatic. "I mean a homestead. I know we need a man for that, but it's a possibility.''

"So where are you going to get a man, if Papa don't come back?''

"I don't know.''

"Maybe I could place an advertisement in the town newsletter: young woman wants man,''—he pretended to be forming the notice in his head—"looks, habits, character not important, but must be old enough to file a homestead.'' He laughed. "Think we'd get any takers?''

"Not if they found out that having to put up with you was a part of the bargain.''

"Ouch! That hurts more than my face.''

"I'll be back as soon as I can.''

"All right," Pablo said, "and I won't even ask you to buy sugar sticks for all of us."

Juanita didn't reply to his jest. There hadn't been any sweets in the Lopez household since the previous Christmas. As she made the mile-long walk to the general store, she pondered their situation. What if their father never did come back? How could she keep the family together? Was it possible for her and Pablo to put enough food on the table or keep a roof over their heads?

A pebble worked its way into her shoe, forcing Juanita to stop and remove the worn-out footgear. The sole was a patchwork of thin leather and a piece of cardboard, not very comfortable, but she didn't like to walk into town without her bonnet and something covering her feet. Bad enough to feel like a beggar, she didn't wish to look like one.

Thinking of the items she would have to purchase caused her stomach to growl. She had not eaten since taking a small portion of the bone meal soup she had made from leftovers the previous night. *We're making leftovers from leftovers,* she lamented to herself, *and we've run out of those!*

Chapter Five

The boardinghouse had only one room available, but it provided two cots and a washstand. Tito and Darby split the price and each staked out a bed for the night.

"Guess I'll see if I can replace the cinch on my saddle," Darby said, once they were settled in. "The strap is so worn and frayed, I'm afraid I'm going to end up sitting in cactus during a sharp turn."

Tito had his gun out, using a lightweight rag to wipe away the granules of dust, which had collected during their many hours of travel. He worked the action and checked to see if it needed any oil. Always a man who kept his gun in perfect working order, he knew the weapon could mean his life at any given moment. "Okay," he said, pausing from his maintenance, "I've got a couple things to pick up at the store."

"Want to meet up at the stable?"

"I'd like to clean up first. How about you check and see where they provide a tub and water?"

"Okay, I'll ask the landlady."

"What do you want to do about supper?"

"I don't like to eat alone, Tito. After you clean up, we could try one of the saloons."

"Sounds good."

Darby left first and Tito finished working with the

gun. He had removed the bullets, so he took a moment to reload. Rising to his feet, he slipped the pistol into the holster. For the next ten minutes, he practiced drawing his gun. Speed was not so important as making the draw a natural reaction. When surprised or under the duress of a sudden fight, Tito knew it was imperative to be able to pull the gun and fire without thinking. To a man whose life might depend on it, the drawing and shooting of his gun had to be a preconditioned habit, as much second nature to him as when a person closed their eyes with a sneeze.

He finally left the gun in the holster, but he did not put the leather thong over the hammer to secure the Colt in its sheath. With men like Puggot after him, he would leave the thong off whenever he was in town or had any possibility of being ambushed. It was not a good feeling.

Tito left the room suffering from a helpless depression. It had taken so many years to finally put the fighting behind him. He had a new life ahead, friends who respected him, a place to call home, a decent job with Wells Fargo. How he hated returning to the days of looking over his shoulder, watching every shadow, afraid it was a trap, and possibly having to kill someone to survive himself. Perhaps it was a cruel twist of fate that this had been thrust upon him. Maybe a man could not outrun his past. Whatever the reason or his destiny, his path was set, he was a target, wary of strangers, unable to put his back to a door or window, forced to be forever ready to kill or be killed. The only consolation about the situation was that it was not new to him. He'd been in such a position many times before.

* * *

Entering onto the town's main street, Juanita spied the man who had stopped Vince from persisting with his pounding of her brother. By coincidence, he was going in the same direction as she. Juanita arrived at the store several steps behind him, but he paused to hold the door open for her. She felt a flush rush to her cheeks from the gentlemanly gesture. Uncomfortable at being so ragged and dirty, she ducked her head, uttered an embarrassed "thank you," and hurried into the store.

Once inside, she went to the shelf where the tins of condensed milk were located. She could not resist sneaking a glance at the man. He was carrying a considerable amount of trail dust, but was clean-shaven, fairly tall for a Mexican, slender in build, with a strong line to his jaw, and a gentleness about his rich, oak-colored eyes. When he spoke to Millie, the store-owner, asking where the soaps were located, his voice was mellow and rich, with no hint of an accent.

She tried not to stare at him. It would have been good manners to thank him for the intervention between Vince and her brother, but she was ashamed to speak to the man. Dressed in a tattered, faded skirt and a bulky, unflattering work blouse, covered in dust from the long walk, and having not found time for a bath recently, she reasoned her appearance was that of a street panhandler.

She quickly picked up the things she needed and took the few items to the counter. Millie gave her a cordial smile of greeting. It vanished at once when Juanita spoke up.

"I'm not sure if I have enough money for everything,'' she explained softly. "I must have the tins of milk for the baby.''

While Millie wasn't on a first-name basis with many of the sharecroppers or squatters, she usually treated everyone fairly. Juanita had only spoken to her when she paid for what little merchandise she could afford. Her father had run up a bill and it was yet unpaid. She hated to enter the store without being able to put something toward what they owed, but it and the trading post were the only stores for buying goods. Zig Authen, who owned the other place, had shown his lack of sympathy to her family earlier that morning. With he and Vince being pals, there was no justice when dealing with his trading post.

"That comes to a dollar and eighty-five cents,'' Millie said.

Juanita was crestfallen. "That much?''

"I don't charge you people more than anyone else.'' Millie was immediately defensive. "I've got to make enough to keep the doors open.''

"I'm sure you are being more than fair,'' Juanita said quickly. "I wasn't complaining about your prices. It's . . . well, I don't have that much money.''

The woman became rigid, a stern expression entering her face. "You did see the sign in the window, the one that says NO CREDIT?''

"Yes, ma'am.''

"It means what it says, señorita. Too many people around here were like your pa. They took advantage of my soft-hearted nature and ran up huge bills— which never got paid. I'm to the point where I can hardly afford to buy more goods. Fact is, some of the established farmers don't like me serving squatter folks at all. They've threatened more than once to take their business elsewhere and leave me busted.''

"I'm sorry," Juanita was sincere. "I know my father owes you a lot of money. Let me see what I can put back."

Millie did not give an inch, waiting for her to decide. Juanita had to have the milk for the baby. But what about the rest of the family? She had to feed them something!

"I'll be with you in a minute, sir," Millie told the stranger, who had stepped up behind Juanita.

"I'm in no rush," he answered. "And if the young lady is short a few cents, you can add it to my total. I'm always glad to lend a hand to someone who has come onto hard times."

Juanita spun about and glowered with indignation. "Excuse me, señor! I am not in the habit of asking for charity!"

He was unmoved by her outburst, meeting her hot stare with a disarming smile. "I was only being neighborly, señorita. I intended no offense." She took a breath, as if to interject something, but he was quick to continue. "I've been through lean times on occasion myself. Accepting a helping hand isn't the same as taking a handout."

The words appeared to buckle her sails, before the wind could blow up a real storm. She faltered before his gaze. "I-I don't know. I don't usually . . ."

Tito placed a half-eagle on the counter. "I'd take it as a favor, if you'd allow me to pay for the little dab of supplies you have there, señorita. I often leave that much extra change for a meal."

Millie was quick to act. She immediately snatched

up the coin and added in the sticks of jerky and shaving soap that Tito had placed next to the girl's stuff. She made change and put Juanita's items into a flour sack.

"Nice to know there are a few Christian people left around here," she said to break the awkward silence between Tito and Juanita. "Thank you, sir, and do come again."

Tito left first, once again holding the door for the young lady. He stuck the jerky into his shirt pocket and carried the jar of soap in his left hand.

"I don't know what to say," the girl said softly. "I wouldn't want you thinking that . . ."

Tito lifted a hand to stop her from continuing. "Don't mention it, señorita. Like I said, I've been short a few coins once or twice myself. I'm glad to be of service."

She looked at him with eyes that were alert, and as bright as polished oak. "I'll simply say thank you then."

"You are very welcome."

Then she ducked away and hurried up the street.

Tito immediately wished he knew the girl's name. However, if he had been bold enough to ask, she might have gotten the wrong idea. He didn't want her thinking he would press his advantage because he had paid for a handful of groceries.

Even as he argued himself out of being forward, he stared after her. She wasn't a dazzling beauty, but she could have been attractive with very little effort. At present, the girl's clothes were dusty from walking the powdery road, and her dress had been mended so many times that the design was lost. Plus, she wore her hair tucked up under an unsightly, worn-out, Quaker-style bonnet. He also noticed that her shoes were thin, with holes worn through, and probably uncomfortable. With all of the negatives, she still had a natural feminine sway to her hips, the movement causing his heart to increase its tempo.

"Whatcha' doing, Pard?" Darby arrived to interrupt his ogling.

"Picked up some soap."

"Shaving soap, huh?" Darby said. "I've been shaving for two years."

"Yeah?" Pacheco looked at his youthful, whiskerless face. "Bet you cut yourself *both* times."

"Funny," he retorted. "You ask the storekeep about the dead guy?"

"It kind of slipped my mind."

"Yeah." Darby took a glance at the girl. "I can see how you could have been preoccupied with other things."

"You find out where we can get a bath?"

"The lady at the boardinghouse said to go over to the tavern. They have a bathhouse round to the back." He grinned. "You didn't get an invite to dinner or something?"

"No."

"Then why the big fuss about taking a bath?"

"When I commence to sharing the same scent as my horse, I figure it's time to rub off a coat of dirt. You might consider doing a little washing yourself."

"I guess it wouldn't hurt, but it's only been a couple weeks. Hate to rinse away the body's natural protection. You know that washing too much allows the miseries to enter a man's body."

"I expect you are on the safe side concerning the miseries."

Darby didn't take offense at the belittling. "You get her name?"

"No."

"Maybe you ain't as lucky as I been thinking, Pacheco."

"Since running into you, I figure my luck has been going nowhere but downhill."

Darby laughed. "Fickle thing about luck, my friend, it can be bad or good."

"I think it's about time I had a little good."

Darby grew serious. "They don't have a telegraph in this town. You think Puggot and his boys would try and follow us this far?"

"It sounded as if Baxter was real fond of his brother. I'd guess he is going to hound us till we have no place to run."

"I've made up my mind. Once I find another job, I ain't going to run. A man can't live his whole life looking back over his shoulder."

Tito took a gander up the street and back down. They were at a distinct disadvantage, not even knowing who to look for. "Wonder if Baxter was as ugly as his brother?"

"Never seen him or any of his men, Pacheco. I had only hired on the first of the month. I was barely getting acquainted with the guys I was working with."

"Once we find someone who knew the dead guy we found, we'll light out for Broken Spoke. I'm pretty certain you can get a job there, and we will have help, should Puggot show up."

"Sounds like a fine idea, Pard, but are you sure the

people of Broken Spoke won't mind us bringing trouble down onto their town?''

''I've friends and a couple cousins there. If Puggot comes looking for trouble, it'll even up the odds. Until then, we'll have to keep our eyes open for any strangers, and that means about everyone.''

''Heck of a way to live, but it beats the alternative—dying.''

Chapter Six

Tito was up early. He wanted to find out what he could about the dead man and put that chore behind him. Darby was also anxious to get moving. Finding the Mexican's body had put a crimp in Tito's idea to take the train from Denver to Cheyenne and return to Broken Spoke. He had thought to erase any possible trail with the move. Running was not something he was used to, but he didn't want to be involved in more killing. He had fought in the Mexican War, during the French occupation, been a guard, a lawman, and had been in several skirmishes while at Broken Spoke. He was tired of fighting and killing. Once Luke Mallory had helped him land the job for Wells Fargo, he had hoped to put an end to making his living with a gun.

He wondered what Mallory would say when he returned home with a pack of gunmen on his trail. The one thing he was sure of, he knew the man would offer to side him. He and Mallory had been in tight spots before, each relying on the other for survival. It would be a relief to reach the relative safety of Broken Spoke.

Stepping off of the porch, he started up the street to visit the deputy and start asking around about the dead man they had found. He spied Vince outside the sheriff's office. He was talking to a rough-looking gent, covered with trail dust, unshaven, and looking as if he hadn't slept in a week. They parted company and Vince walked away. That should have been the end of it, but the stranger came directly at Tito.

"Pacheco!" the man said with a snarl, his hand streaking for his gun, "you're a dead man!"

Tito reacted instantly, clawing at his own pistol. He knew he would be too slow. As the man cleared leather, Tito dropped to one knee and whipped his gun into play.

The blast from the assailant's gun seemed to go off right in his face, but the scream of the bullet sang harmlessly past his ear. Tito returned fire, a split-second before the man could shoot again. The impact from his slug jarred the man and ruined his aim for a second shot. He sagged forward, still working to pull the trigger again.

The assailant fired once more, but the bullet kicked up dirt three feet in front of Tito. However, there was no need to shoot at the man again. Tito rose slowly to a standing position as the attacker slumped to the ground. He groaned once, then lay still.

Vince came running over, his gun out, searching about to see what had happened. He skidded to a stop next to the body of the attacker. He looked up from him to Tito and realized the fight was over.

"Good gadfry, Pacheco! I knew you was trouble on the hoof."

"It wasn't my fault, Deputy!" Tito exclaimed. "I never saw this hombre before."

"So why'd he try to kill you?"

"I don't know."

Vince studied the man for a moment, prodded the

lifeless form with the toe of his boot, and gave a negative shake of his head. "He asked me if I knew you. Soon as I pointed you out, he tries to gun you down. I'd say you ain't exactly been straight with me."

"I'm telling you, I don't know who he is."

Vince holstered his gun and put his hands on his hips. "Be that as it may, Pacheco, I'll take your gun. The judge will have to decide the matter."

Tito didn't have any options. He removed his gun and belt and handed them to Vince. With a last look at the body, he wondered if the dead man was Baxter Puggot. It would be a relief to stop running, providing he didn't end up in prison for defending himself.

Juanita was surprised to see the strange man at her door. He was young, perhaps not much older than her own eighteen years. When she stepped out to see what he wanted, he removed his hat to reveal thick, curly black hair.

"Would this be the Lopez place?"

"Yes, I'm Juanita Lopez."

He paused to look around. Gena and Maria were sitting on the ground, playing with sticks and rocks, pretending the items were table dressings. Ruban and Rick were making repairs to the fence that housed their cow. The baby was asleep for her morning nap, lying in the cradle, just inside the door.

"Quite a bunch of you," the man said.

"Six and the baby."

"My name's Darby. I think you might have met the fellow I've been traveling with, the one who helped stop the fight between your brother and the deputy, then ran into again at the store yesterday?"

"Yes, of course, I remember."

Darby lowered his head, as if unable to look her in the eye. "I've some bad news."

Juanita felt a queasy churn within her stomach. "Bad news?"

"The reason we came to Ivory Flats is that we ran into a fellow a few miles outside of a place called Helpful, over Colorado way. The old boy had run his horse into a prairie dog city and got busted up in a fall. He was already dead from his injuries before we found him. About all we could do was see that he was buried proper." He sighed, and continued. "The guy was Mexican, probably in his midforties, and he had a white topknot, a gray streak in his hair that ran from front to back."

Juanita sucked in her breath.

"He wasn't carrying anything but this old watch"— Darby held out the timepiece—"seven cents, and a piece of paper. We deciphered that the first name might begin with an *H*."

"Hermando was my father's first name," she murmured softly. "He went to look for us a new place to live. He . . ." She had to swallow the sob which rose in her throat. "I'm sorry."

"No, señorita." Darby excused her show of emotion. "I'm the one who is sorry to have to bring you such bad news."

Juanita silently took the watch and the seven cents. "Thank you for the information," she managed to say. "We might never have known what happened to him."

"Pacheco and I have been searching the past few

days, trying to find someone who knew the dead man. I'm plum regretful over your loss.''

"The man at the store.'' She held back her sorrow. "His name is Pacheco?''

"Yeah, he'd have come out here with me, but he got into a gunfight this morning.''

"Gunfight?''

"Some man threw down on him right in the street. If the other guy hadn't missed his first shot, Pacheco would be getting sized for a wooden box.''

"Is he all right?'' she asked, suddenly finding his welfare more important than the fact that Hermando would not be coming back.

"They locked him up. I was told you have a judge in this here town. He's going to rule on the fight. Can't see him calling it anything but self-defense. After all, the other guy drew first.''

"You don't know Judge Lockard. He is very strict about enforcing the law. If I had told him about Vince beating up my brother, he might have taken his badge. I hope Mr. Pacheco makes a good impression.''

"I'm sure he will.''

"Why did the man attack him?''

"We don't know for certain, but there's a chance it has to do with another shooting over in Fallwood. I would be dead, except for Pacheco lending a hand. I owe him my life.''

Juanita was surprised by that. She had seen a gentle side to the man, the way he had been tactful enough to pay for her goods without making her feel indebted to him. Now she learned that he had ridden for days to pass on news of her father's death, plus he had saved another man's life.

"What else can you tell me about Mr. Pacheco?"

Darby began to talk. Juanita listened intently, her grief over losing her father suppressed for the moment. She had to make some hard, fast decisions. If it became known that there was no man in the Lopez household, the family would be split up. She had seen that before, the separation of orphaned children, often given to anyone who would care for them, never to see their brothers or sisters again. There was little chance anyone would want to take on the responsibility of seven new kids all at once. She had to think fast. No matter what steps she had to take, she was going to keep that from happening to herself and the children!

It was only a small group assembled in the church for the court hearing. Most people had work to do and few had any interest in the death of a complete stranger. The judge, however, took his position very seriously. He was stern and cold in outward appearance. Vince had warned Tito that Lockard, although semiretired, was one tough character.

Judge Lockard brought the meeting to order and proceeded to ask Vince the circumstances surrounding the shooting of a man in the street of their fair town. He then listened to all other witnesses, before he finally set his steely gaze on Tito.

"What do you have to say for yourself, young man?" he asked.

Tito rose to his feet. "I don't know who the man was, your honor. He called me by name, so I can only guess he was sent here by Baxter Puggot."

"And you killed the brother of this Baxter Puggot?"

"During a card game in Fallwood. He drew down on an unarmed man. I had to shoot him to save that man's life."

A dark frown furrowed Lockard's brow. "So you have killed other men?"

"I've been forced to defend myself on more than one occasion, Your Honor."

The judge paused to look over a piece of paper on his desk. "I see you also brought information on the death on one of our local citizens, Hermando Lopez?"

"Yes, sir, we found his body off of the main trail, about twenty miles from Helpful, over Colorado way."

"So, when we look at the tally, one man dies in a card game, another man is dead along the trail, and now a third man is killed on the main street of our town. It would seem that death follows you, Mr. Pacheco. Are you attempting to live up to your reputation?"

"Reputation?"

"I took the time to wire the authorities in Wyoming about you. It seems you have been involved in several killings over around the town of Broken Spoke."

"There was a range war at the time, Judge. I was acting on behalf of the law. You can check with Jack Cole, the acting town marshal."

"I believe you made a little noise in Mexico too. Do you deny being listed as an enemy of the state there?"

"I was one of the countrymen who sided with Maximilian, back when the French government was in power, Judge. The civil war ended a dozen years back.''

''You must have only been a boy.''

''A war forces a man to grow up rather sudden,'' Tito replied. ''I was seventeen when I left Mexico.''

''It appears that violence has accompanied you for most of your life, Mr. Pacheco.''

Tito did not reply, lowering his head. He had to admit that his luck had been on the deadly side as of late. Three deaths in less than a week's time. It could start people to wondering about him.

''What is your occupation?''

''I work for Wells Fargo at the moment.''

''I would have thought you were nothing more than a wandering saddle tramp with a gun.''

''No, sir,'' Tito replied. ''I've a good job.''

''But you killed a man at the gaming tables?''

''It was either him or one of us at the table. Like I said, the man he drew down on didn't have a gun to defend himself.''

''So, a gunfighter, a gambler, and a Wells Fargo employee.'' Lockard grunted his contempt. ''I'm surprised that Wells Fargo doesn't have better sense in whom they hire. We don't need your kind in Kansas, son. We've had enough blood to last us into the next century.''

''The man on the street tried to kill me, Judge. I only shot back to save my own life.''

''So you claim.'' He cleared his throat and held Tito with searing eyes. ''I believe you need a change of scenery, Mr. Pacheco. We don't intend to tolerate gunfights on our main street. Perhaps a couple years behind bars will give you a new perspective on life.''

"Your honor, I—"

"As you have no responsibilities in the world," he cut him off, "I think it prudent to treat this matter with a degree of severity." He continued to glower, his face like a mask of granite. "Two years behind bars ought to give you ample time to reflect upon your quickness to use a gun."

Tito was stunned. He couldn't believe his ears. Two years in prison for defending his own life?

"Unless someone has something to add, it is the judgment of this court that—"

"Excuse me, Your Honor!" A young lady prevented him from continuing. Tito recognized the girl as the one he had helped at the general store. She had a bundle in her arms and displayed an obvious embarrassment. "May I speak to you?"

The judge displayed a frown at being interrupted. "You have something to say, Miss Lopez?"

"Yes, Your Honor," she said quietly. "I . . . could I speak to you privately?"

"Is this pertinent to the case before us?"

"Yes, it most certainly is."

"Very well, approach the bench and explain."

The young woman shifted the bundle in her arms. From the muffled sounds, Tito knew she had a baby in the blanket. She made her way up to stand before the judge. She spoke in hushed tones, turned the baby to where Lockard could see it, and suddenly appeared very ashamed. In fact, Tito could see a red glow about her cheeks. He felt a glimmer of hope that she was coming to his defense. After all, he had stuck up for her brother, then paid for a few items she needed at the store. It made sense, but when she finished speaking, Lockard fixed an intense stare on him that was anything but friendly.

"Mr. Pacheco, would you come forward?"

Tito was puzzled, but approached the bench and stopped, standing next to the girl. He glanced at her from the corner of his eye, but she would not look at him. He met the hostile glare on the face of the judge. It was enough of a scowl to ward off a grizzly bear. Tito had no idea as to what was going on, but a chill raced up his spine.

"It has come to the court's attention that you know the young lady here, Mr. Pacheco."

"I bumped into her earlier," Tito explained.

The glare worsened. "What a delightful way you have with words" he rasped cynically. "I wonder if you also know the two short words a gentleman uses when he weds his bride."

Tito blinked at such a question. "I do?"

"Those are the words, Mr. Pacheco," he said. As Tito stood there in bewilderment, Lockard put his attention on the girl. "And what do you say, Juanita Lopez? Do you also take this man to be your lawfully wedded husband?"

"Yes, I do," the young lady said quietly.

A crate of fireworks exploded in Tito's head. He opened his mouth, but the link to his voice had been severed. He was unable to muster forth any words.

"By the authority vested in me, I pronounce you man and wife." The judge glared at Tito. "You may kiss the bride."

Juanita positioned the baby in the crook of one arm and swung around toward Tito. Before he could get his mental faculties working, she came up onto her toes and gave him a quick peck on the lips. The few spectators in the room mumbled their questions to one another about the bizarre turn of events.

Tito was dumbfounded, totally bewildered at what had taken place. Juanita hooked her free arm into his and Judge Lockard again cleared his throat.

"Upon final review, the court finds that Tito Pacheco acted in self-defense. There are no charges to be filed against him at this time. He is free to take his wife and child and return to their home." With that, he hammered his gavel on the desk to dismiss the hearing.

Chapter Seven

Once outside, Tito looked around for Darby. This whole deal had an odor about it, and it smelled to the heavens like his doing.

"Inez has your eyes," Juanita said after a moment, making light of the situation.

"My eyes!" His voice returned with a vengeance. "I don't know Inez! I never saw her before!" He whirled about and glared at her. "And I don't know you either, señorita! What kind of ridiculous story did you tell that judge?"

The girl flinched under his verbal assault. "You sound upset."

"Oh, do I?" He laughed with contempt. "I can't imagine why. I start out with a solid case of self-defense in a shooting and I end up married! What kind of loco farm is Lockard running?"

She lowered her eyes and voice both. "He thinks that you are Inez's father."

"What?" He was beyond comprehension. "Why would he think that?"

"I told him that you and I were"—she swallowed hard and ducked her head—"more than friends."

"Talk about the egg coming before the chicken! I

61

never set eyes on you before I rode into town. There's no way I could be the father of that child!"

"Of course, she isn't yours!" The girl's voice was at once defensive. "She isn't mine either! She's my little sister."

The words hit him like a slap across the face. Tito didn't know if he had misplaced several key cards to his playing deck, or if it was the woman who needed some real help sorting her hand. The confusion slowed his burning fuse while he attempted to make sense of the situation.

"What am I missing?" he mumbled inanely. "Didn't you just tell the judge the baby was ours? Isn't that why he tricked me into marrying you?"

"Would you rather have gone to prison for two years?" She tossed the words back at him. "If I hadn't spoken up on your behalf, you'd have been sent to jail."

"There's a sound logic, I either serve a couple years in prison, or I end up with a life sentence with you."

His curt remark caused her head to lift and instilled burning embers into the woman's eyes. "I'm sorry, señor! I didn't know I was such an ugly and undesirable witch that a man would prefer prison to me!"

Tito gulped down a sizable swallow of humble stew. "I didn't mean for it to sound like—"

"I owed you a debt," she said defensively. "I was trying to pay you back."

"I think two dollars would have covered it."

"Listen, Mr. Pacheco, you are married to me proper. If you run out on me, Judge Lockard will put a bounty on your head for desertion. You had better start thinking of how to make the best of this arrangement.''

Tito shoved his hands into his pockets and bowed his shoulders in defeat. ''Married a lousy two minutes and I'm already henpecked.''

Juanita shifted the baby to a comfortable position and placed her hand gently on his arm. ''If you'll give me a chance to explain, I know you'll understand the logic behind our marriage of convenience.''

''Convenient for whom?''

She ignored the barb. ''I have to think of Inez, Mr. Pacheco. I have two other sisters, Gena and Maria. You helped my brother, Pablo, when you stopped Vince from beating on him yesterday. My other two brothers are Ruban and Ricardo. I had to have a man to head up our family or the town fathers would split us up, give away my younger brothers and sisters to anyone who would take them. They would all end up raised in different homes, perhaps never to see one another again.''

''What are you talking about?''

The news you brought about finding a dead man''— she took a deep breath—''it was my father, Hermando Lopez. My mother died giving Inez life. The midwife said she was too along in years to be having children. As the oldest member of the family, it's up to me to keep the children together. I intend to do that, whatever it takes.''

''Even if it means marrying a complete stranger.''

''Yes.''

''What about my feelings, señorita? Don't you think I ought to have been given the choice of marriage or going to jail?''

"Mr. Darby assured me that you would rather be married."

"Somehow I knew this was going to end up with him being involved." Tito swept the area with a critical glance. Not surprisingly, Darby was nowhere to be seen.

"You would have been sent to prison, Mr. Pacheco. It can't be any worse to be a temporary father to a few children for a year or two."

"If you and Pablo are an example, I'm not so sure about that."

"Look at the baby," she held Inez out for him to see. "Could you stand by and see such a beautiful little girl given to a stranger, never to know what happened to her brothers and sisters?"

The tiny face was as peaceful and precious as anything Tito had ever seen in his life. He suspected the innocent baby purposely displayed an angelic expression to convince him. However, what the girl said did sink in. He had known families that had been split up after the death of the parents. During the war in Mexico, he had seen a great number of children without parents, some without friends or relatives to take them in. Many of the abandoned or orphaned kids ended up in a life of servitude, working for anyone who would offer them shelter or food. He uttered a sigh of defeat.

"What about your reputation and mine? How many people around here are going to think this child is ours?"

The shame returned to her face. "I-I don't know."

"I don't suppose Darby told you about why that gunman came looking for me?"

"Not exactly."

"Well, it's likely that there will be more of them. The brother of the man I was forced to kill will keep looking for me. Do you want to put your life and the lives of your brothers and sisters in the middle of that?"

"You don't have to remain in Ivory Flats, Mr. Pacheco."

"What do you mean?"

"Once we come to some sort of agreement, you can leave here. No one will stop you."

"An agreement?"

"So long as you are alive, no one will break up our family. With a little help, Pablo and I can manage the household. I've been taking in laundry, and Pablo is old enough to hold down a real job. My only concern is to keep a roof over our head, and for us to remain a family."

The dawn broke; Tito understood. "So that's it." He had to chuckle at her shrewd thinking. "I see your plan now. You only needed a title for yourself. With you being my wife, you can keep all of the children together. It doesn't matter if I leave town or what I do, so long as I don't get myself killed."

"And it will save you a prison term."

He studied her closely. It put her ill at ease to the point where she lowered the lash-adorned lids to hide her shimmering black eyes.

"The judge called you Juanita."

"That's my name."

Tito rubbed his jaw thoughtfully. "Now that I think about it, he seemed quite familiar with you."

"What are you saying?"

"If I was going to wager a bet on it, I'd say he knows the baby there isn't yours or mine."

She squirmed under his knowing scrutiny. "Mr. Pacheco, I—"

"So what else do you want from me, besides my last name?"

The change of subject allowed her to hold her head up once more. "I only wish to save our home. As I said, Pablo and I will get jobs as soon as we can."

Tito gave consideration to his options. He could leave the woman and ride out. The marriage had been a farce. It wouldn't take much explaining to get a different judge to issue an annulment to his so-called wedding vows. There was also the worry of Baxter Puggot or another of his henchmen showing up. He needed to make some decisions. His first was that he didn't wish to run forever. He would probably have to face Baxter one day. If the man he killed was one of his hired guns, Baxter was bound to follow him to Ivory Flats. The threat of his arrival was now going to be a concern to this girl and her family. He didn't know how far Baxter would go to find him, but she and the kids could easily become targets.

"Juanita Lopez, huh?" he said, putting his attention back on her.

A flush rose into her cheeks. "I guess it's Mrs. Pacheco now, at least for a little while."

The name had a strange, yet oddly beautiful sound to it. Tito glanced over her from bonnet to shoes. She was trim, moderately attractive, even while her clothes were nothing more than patches over patches. One thing he really hated was the Quaker bonnet. A proper senorita should have a brightly colored scarf or straw hat. She and her brothers and sisters were about one step above ragged little beggars.

"I'm sorry about your father."

"He was never a strong man. Mother ran the house, but she was unable to stop his drinking or gambling. We worked the entire season picking beans, my father, Pablo, Ricky, and myself. He took a pay voucher and went to find us a new home."

"We didn't find any money on him."

"It's quite possible he gambled it away," she said, without any condemnation. "He claimed he would find a place for us to live, perhaps even our own homestead. He was not very good at keeping his word."

Tito took a final look around. He could only assume that Baxter's man had arrived in Ivory Flats alone. It was worrisome not knowing the face of his enemy. Any stranger could be another of Baxter's men, or even Puggot himself. It made no sense to sit back like a target and wait to be shot down without warning. Second, he had no right to get a young girl's family involved in his troubles, even if she had been the one to initiate contact. However, he did know of one place they would be safe, a place where he had friends to help—Broken Spoke.

"What are you going to do?" Juanita asked, in little more than a whisper.

"I think we'll order you a bath."

At her incredulous expression, he might have just dumped a handful of mud down her neck. She pulled back a step and gave a shake of her head. "A bath?"

"Can't have you running around like a street urchin."

"A what?"

"First off, let's go over to the store and pay off your family debt. Tito Pacheco doesn't owe money to anyone." He gave her another quick once-over. "While we're there, we can pick you out a dress and new shoes." He critically eyed her headgear. "And a scarf or something."

Juanita's eyes grew wide. "You can't be serious!"

"You heard me." He lifted his chin importantly. "If you're going to be Mrs. Pacheco, you have to maintain a certain status. Your debt is my debt, and I always pay my debts. As for the way you're dressed, I certainly can't take you to Broken Spoke looking like a beggar."

"Broken Spoke?"

"I have a plot of land there. Not much of a house, but it's easily as good as some of the shanties I've seen around here."

She stared at him agape, as if unable to believe the words Tito was saying. The tears that misted her eyes added to their brightness. It warmed him inside, an experience he had not felt in many years. It was as if a cold, vacant room had suddenly been heated by a cheerful, crackling fire.

"I-I'm sorry, but I couldn't let you buy me new clothes." She hardly breathed the words. "I mean, the children need so much. It wouldn't be . . ."

But Tito raised a hand to silence her objections. "One of the first rules of being my wife, Juanita, is that you let me do some of the thinking. I may not be ready to take on being a big family man just yet, but I do know what to expect from a wife. It's important for a man to be proud of his woman, not ashamed to have her show her face in public."

"Whatever you say, Mr. Pacheco."

"Tito," he corrected her. "The name is Tito."

"All right, Tito." She murmured the name.

"I tend to favor pink, yellow, or light blues."

Presently, she reminded him of how a small child must look on Christmas morning. Her smile radiated ardor and her misty eyes glowed with an unfamiliar emotion.

"I-I can't tell you what . . ." Her voice cracked. "I'm sorry, I don't wish to . . ."

"No need to make a big fuss over it, Juanita. It's my reputation that's on the line here. Can't have people thinking I'm not a decent provider."

She shifted the baby into her left arm and hooked her right through his own. It instilled in him a sense of pride. He ought to be fuming over Juanita being involved in a ploy with Lockard. They had used trickery and deceit to trap him in a pretense wedding. However, those feelings were overshadowed by a satisfied and pleasing sensation. He could muster no outrage at finding himself tricked into a phony marriage, and the fires of anger had been doused. Curiously, there wasn't even any smoke left behind.

Chapter Eight

Baxter Puggot looked around the saloon. Everyone was back but Quint. He recalled the direction he had gone was south into Kansas. There was a chance that he would be a day longer returning than the rest. However, Nolen had already hit town. The two of them should have been about an equal distance from Fallwood.

What do you think?'' Nolen asked, probably thinking along the same lines. "Not one of us got a line on that drifter. Should we follow after Quint?''

"Why would Quint have any better luck?''

"You know how he thinks, Bax. He'll follow the horses. A good many men can blend in when they enter a town, but most liverymen or stable hostlers know each and every animal that enters their barn. I'd lay my odds that Quint has been tracking the palomino horse the Mexican was riding. I'll bet you a meal he's on the trail of that animal right now.''

"So why haven't we heard from him?''

"Maybe he hasn't been able to find a way to get word to us. Could be, he's out in some farming or ranching community where there isn't any telegraph.''

"We shouldn't have let him go alone into Kansas. He is too bullheaded for his own good. If he caught up with those two, he would likely try and take them on by himself," Baxter said.

"I hope not. The men who saw the shooting all swear that Pacheco fellow was real quick getting his gun clear. He was sitting down, yet he cleared leather and killed your brother before Saul could shoot down the kid."

"Saul was no gunman, Nolen. He couldn't have beat half the women in this town to the draw. He was always talking about guns, but he didn't practice. He used my rep to make men back down and respect him. They knew that to mess with him was to end up fighting me."

"Except no one told this guy, Pacheco."

Baxter gritted his teeth, the veins along his temples became pronounced, and his face grew dark and cold with his rage.

"I'm going to watch that man die hard! I want to put a bullet in him and watch him twist and squirm in pain. I want him to know he's dying. Then, when he's on the brink of death, I'm going to spit in his face!"

"What if Quint takes him out?"

"Then I'll bust his head! I made it clear I wanted to see the Mexican drop myself."

Nolen removed his timepiece and looked at it. "Be dark pretty soon. I doubt that Quint will make it back tonight."

"We'll give him till noon tomorrow."

"Whatever you say, Bax. You're the boss."

Baxter brooded in silence, staring out the window. He could see nothing stirring for miles, but he kept looking. Somewhere, there were two men running loose, the two men responsible for his brother's death.

In all honesty, Saul hadn't been much of a man, but he and Baxter had always been close. After the death of their father, Baxter had raised Saul like his son. He was six years younger than Baxter and never questioned his leadership. They had done a lot of hunting and fishing together. They had been the best of friends. Now Saul was dead, killed by an act of stupidity. What a waste.

Turning his attention to his next action, Baxter worried that Quint might have gotten himself into trouble. Nolen's evaluation about the man was correct. Quint knew to follow a man's horse. Once he learned which animal he was looking for, he would track it to the ends of the earth. The problem was, he didn't know when to back off. Pacheco had been lucky to take out Saul. If his luck held, he might also have gotten Quint. If that was the case, news would reach him and his boys soon enough.

Considering his men, Baxter went over them in his mind. Nolen had gotten on the wrong side of the law at one time and joined the gang a year back. He was smart, someone he could count on for council, but he didn't have the innards for their kind of hunting. It was hard to believe, but he even felt sorry for their killing a couple red savages. What kind of bounty hunter had a conscience about heathen Indians?

Moving on, he considered the others. Chiggers was a half-breed mix, Negro and white, the illegitimate son of a black slave woman. He didn't talk much, but he was full of hate and solid in any kind of fight. Trapper, Marx, and Walt had been in and out of prison and hated real jobs. The three of them were all in their late twenties or early thirties, had no homes, and were good with their guns. Baxter led the gang because he was the most ruthless of the bunch. They all enjoyed the hunt, except for Nolen, and even Nolen liked the money. Pacheco might stretch his luck and either escape from or kill Quint. If so, his luck would run out real quick, once they caught up with him. They would butcher him like a squealing pig!

Judge Lockard was out in his yard, cutting the dead blossoms off of a large rose bush when Tito approached him. He glanced up and grumbled something under his breath. Tito didn't catch the exact words, but it was obvious the judge was not surprised to see him.

"Collecting dead flowers, Judge?"

"Removing the dried and wilted blossoms promotes new buds to open. The more you tend to the rose bush, the more flowers will bloom."

"Little late in the year. I doubt many of the new buds will have time to open before winter sets in."

"I've had a few blossoms as late as mid-November. Only thing that slows these flowers down is freezing weather."

"Don't see many flowers where I come from."

"In Wyoming?"

"We get a few, but there isn't a real long growing season for flowers—crops either, for that matter."

"Speaking of flowers, how is the new bride and baby?"

"You know the baby isn't Juanita's, don't you?"

He straightened up and began to remove his work gloves. "She needed some time to recover, son. You brought news of the death of her pa. She came and asked if I could help her keep the family together.''

"And you thought a good way of doing that was to blackmail me into marrying her?''

Instead of being indignant or denying it, the judge chuckled. "Not a bad idea, huh?''

"Except that I had no say in the matter. What am I supposed to do with a wife and six kids?''

"Not a thing.''

Tito stared at him blankly. "Say what?''

"I'll issue an annulment one week from today and you will again be footloose and free as a tumbleweed. As I said, Juanita asked for a few days to find a way to hold her family together. She's a smart girl. If she and the two older boys can find a little work, they just might get by.''

"Big undertaking for a girl and a couple kids.''

"It they can't manage it, I'll have to appoint guardians for each of the children.'' He sighed. "I told her she could have the week to get things sorted out. The pretense of your name will prevent anyone from getting too excited about splitting up the family. There are a few around town who would want the boys for the free labor offered, and more than one couple would like the baby. Some of the others would have more trouble finding a home.''

"I can't see Juanita and the two boys earning much of a living.''

"Like I said, I gave her a week to try, but I won't watch those kids up and starve.''

"And I'm supposed to sit here for a week, then take the annulment papers and forget this all happened?''

"Something like that. You did say you worked for Wells Fargo?"

"Yes."

"Well, there you are. If you don't want to stick around, that's fine. I'm the only one who will know that Juanita is not legally wed. So long as she and the boys can keep a roof over their heads and food on the table, I won't interfere. The idea is not to break up the family, not if we can help it."

"You might have had the courtesy to bring me in on this ruse. It was quite a shock, the way you tricked me into saying I do."

"I didn't think you would go along with it," the judge replied. "After all, you said some men were after you."

"And it puts all those kids in danger."

He took on a serious expression. "If they were my kids, I'd sure see that they were not caught up in harm's way. Maybe you could take them away from here, locate them in a different town or something. Be a real shame if anything bad happened and they were caught in the middle."

Tito could see the wheels turning in the old man's head. "So that's it, huh? You expect me to take them with me, set them up with a place of their own, maybe even find jobs for Juanita and the boys. Then if I get killed, they will have my name and a place to live."

"Good thinking, son. I never even thought about that." He showed several stumps, which were all that remained of his teeth, in a wide grin. "Now that you bring it up, it would make a lot of sense. Darby said you had a homestead, one that you were going to lose claim to over in Broken Spoke, because you were never there to make improvements.''

"Somehow, I knew Darby's name was going to enter into this scheme before we were finished.''

"Seems a worthwhile young man.''

"But not worthwhile enough to volunteer to marry Juanita himself.''

Lockard chuckled. "No, not that worthwhile.''

"All right, I see your strategy, Judge. I'm not real pleased at being saddled with a wife and six kids, but I'll do the Christian thing.''

"I've heard that Wells Fargo hired only men of the highest caliber. I will be able to attest to that fact in the future.''

"Yeah, well don't forget the annulment.''

"I shall make out the proper form and have it delivered to Broken Spoke. You will be a free man by the end of the month.''

Tito nodded his head. There was nothing else to say, not even so-long or good-bye. He cursed his luck under his breath and walked away.

It was after Tito had left that all the kids gathered around Juanita to await her explanation.

"Mighty good meal,'' Pablo said.

"First time I've been full in a month,'' Ruban added.

"Me too,'' Rick joined in. "How did you get the guy to bring us all dinner?''

"And how about the new dress?'' Gena asked. "It's sure pretty.''

Juanita looked at each and then sighed deeply. "Mr. Pacheco is my husband. We were married today.''

Pablo and Rick stared at Juanita with their mouths open. Ruban only grinned, as if he thought something was very funny. The girls were too young to really understand what Juanita had told them, other than for Gena, and the baby began to fuss, so she hurried over to see what was the matter.

"You're not kiddin' us?" Rick was first to regain his composure. "You actually married some guy?"

"He's the one who saved me from a beating," Pablo told the others. "And didn't he also lend you the money at the store?"

"Yes, he's the same man."

"Fast romance," he declared. "Maybe the beating from Vince damaged my memory, but I don't recall all of the courting and romance that usually comes *before* the wedding. Did I miss something?"

"Maybe it was love at first sight," Rick joked.

Juanita put up with the teasing, but she remained serious. "It's so we can keep the family together. Pa wasn't gone a week before people were looking to take some of us in like so many stray puppies. I've been approached by one of the farmers and two different women in town. They all wanted to take some of you away from our family and stick you in other people's homes. They would have split us up, all of us!"

"They couldn't do that," Ruban said.

Pablo gave a nod of his head. "Once they knew Pa was dead, they could!"

"So what does Mr. Pacheco think of all this?" Ricky asked. "Is he going to be your real husband?"

"He bought us the food we ate tonight," Pablo said. "But what about tomorrow?"

"I'm not sure what else he has in mind, but at least we can stay together. I'm legally his wife, so I am now responsible for all of you."

"And when he leaves?" Pablo asked.

"We'll worry about that when it comes to pass."

"I heard about Mr. Pacheco from some other kids," Ruben spoke up. "They said he is running from a bunch of killers, and he'll be dead in a week. They said the guy he shot was only a scout or something, and the others would be coming to kill him. Is that true, Sis?"

Pablo narrowed his gaze. "Is it?"

"Mr. Pacheco told me there were some men on his trail, angry over him killing the brother of one of them. I don't know how he intends to deal with it, but he will."

"Sounds like you think a lot of him," Pablo surmised.

"He's her husband," Ricky said and laughed. "She has to defend him now."

"I want you all to get ready for bed. If Mr. Pacheco comes back this evening, I'll need some time to talk to him alone."

"Talk?" Ricky continued to chuckle. "What kind of newly married folks sit around and talk?"

"Ricky!"

He ducked, as if he expected Juanita to swing at him or throw something in his direction. "I was only funning you!" he said, laughing. "I'm going to bed." He started to pull off his shirt. "See? I'm going, I'm going!"

"You too, Ruben."

Both boys hurried to do as they were told, but Pablo

remained with Juanita. He still had some swelling about his face, and his eye was a sickly yellow-brown color. When he spoke, all joking was aside.

"You should have told me what you were up to, big sister," he said in a hushed voice. "What if you've jumped into a buggy with a crazy killer?" He stared into her eyes. "Worse for you, what if this guy wants to make like you two are really married? I mean, are you ready for that?"

"He is a gentleman, an honorable man. I know it."

"I believe some said that about Quantrill, before the war. You remember what he did to Lawrence, Kansas."

"I'm sure this will work out, Pablo. Let me handle it."

"Okay, Sis, whatever you say." He took a step and hesitated. "But remember, you and I can figure a way to keep our family together. We don't need anyone else. If we have to, we can do it alone."

She smiled. "Thanks, Pablo, but it'll be all right. Trust me."

Chapter Nine

Tito sat at the table and stared at his half-empty glass of beer. He was so engrossed in his own thoughts that he wasn't aware of Darby coming over to stand opposite him. When he finally looked up, the young cowboy grinned.

"This isn't where I pictured a man spending his honeymoon night."

"I'm not sure whether to thank you or put a bullet in you."

Darby slid back a chair and sat down. "It wasn't my doing," he explained quickly. "The whole thing came about when I went out to tell her about her father. There was already word spreading about the hearing and she came up with an idea to help."

"Yeah, big help."

"I didn't know what the judge was going to do. The girl said he was a tough nut."

"And you naturally told her what an excellent husband and father I would make."

"About the only clue I had as to what was in her mind was when she asked if you were married. I remembered you telling me that you had no close ties to anyone."

"What about the pack of killers on our trail? Did that enter your thick skull?"

"She told me she only needed a marriage to keep the kids under one roof. She said that once the people in town thought she was legally wed, then you could leave and any judge would have the marriage annulled for you. In essence, the whole sham was only to give her custody of the kids."

Tito sighed. "Yeah, she told me the same thing."

"So no harm done."

"Yeah, she'd be a great provider, all by herself."

"She said her brothers were old enough to work."

"Winter is coming on. One boy is sixteen, another is fourteen, and all of the other kids are younger than that. It takes a lot of supplies to feed a family that size, plus their shack will need a lot of heating fuel to get through the winter. Kansas isn't known for its abundance of wood."

"No, I guess not."

"I did a little asking around. There are over a dozen grown men in Ivory Flats searching for a job to get them through till spring. You saw how popular the boy was during his fight with the deputy. Squatters, vagrants, beggars, that's what the people think of the Lopez family. If I ride out, one or more of those kids will starve or die of exposure this winter, maybe all of them."

"You ain't thinking of taking on the whole family for real?"

Tito toyed with the glass of beer. He had never grown a fondness for the drink. In fact, he seldom drank, even when playing cards. He enjoyed a glass of wine on occasion, but beer or hard liquor did not really suit his taste.

"Did you hear me? I said, you ain't thinking of taking on this pack of lost pups?"

Tito started, unaware that he had drifted off into his own private world again. "You should have seen those kids gobble up the fresh bread we picked up at the bakery. I passed out sugar sticks and you'd think I had given them each a handful of gold."

"There are a good many starving families around, plenty of orphans and needy children too, Tito. You can't take them all under your wing."

Tito knew Darby was telling it straight. There would always be worthwhile people who had come onto a run of bad luck. A man had to know when he could help and when to look away. It was more than a human could endure to try and solve everyone's problems. But this family was no longer part of the nameless faces in the crowd. They weren't the dirty little beggars trying to sell him matches or flowers on the street. These kids had touched him personally. He had seen their faces light up in delight for simply bringing them a stick of candy. He had shared food at their table, even held the baby when she took her bottle.

"I'm going to take them to Broken Spoke," he announced.

"Puggot will come looking, Pard," Darby warned. "You know he'll track you down."

"If he comes looking for vengeance, he had best bring his whole army. I have friends there, men of courage and honor. I won't be in the battle alone."

Darby tipped back his hat. "Well, don't you beat

all!'' He laughed. ''I figured you for a loner, I sure did. You act like a totally independent man. I mean, you ride for miles without a word, often seeming to forget that I'm even around. Now you tell me that you have actual friends. I'm impressed.''

''I told you about the homestead.''

''Yeah, a pile of rocks, you said.''

''It's barren ground, with nothing but a shack on it, but there are a few improvements I can make. With some animals and planting the best five or ten acres, it might be enough to support a family.''

''What about the girl? Have you talked to her about this?''

''Not yet.''

Darby grinned again. ''I'd sure like to be around to see the look on her face. You got any idea how she'll react?''

''No.''

''I could tell that, underneath the dirt and rags, she's a pretty little thing, but she is still a woman. You know they don't think along straight lines like we do.''

''Meaning?''

''Well, she might think you want to make a real marriage out of this, you know the kind where a man and woman share the same goals, the same house,''— he furrowed his brow for dramatic significance—''the same bed.''

''I'll make it clear that we are avoiding any commitment concerning the pretense wedding. I'm not going to push her into something.''

''Mighty big of you, considering she is the one who trapped you into the marriage.''

''I can understand why she did it. Had she come to

me with the idea, I might have gone along with it to start with.''

"Seven kids is a big undertaking, Pard. I hope you're up to the task.''

Tito nodded, but the first task facing him was to suggest the idea to Juanita. He knew Darby was right about how a man and a woman often saw things different. He might see this as an innocent and humane gesture, but she might think he was trying to get her in a position to exercise his husbandly prerogatives.

"When we leaving?'' Darby asked.

"We?''

"I've no place to go at the moment. Unless you have some objections, I'll tag along.'' He lifted a careless shoulder. "If Puggot comes looking, I'd as soon be at your side. I ain't afraid to admit that I don't fancy taking him on alone. I've seen you use that widow-maker on your hip, so I know you and I together would have a chance. I'm not in the same class as you with a gun, but I'll stick for a fight.''

"I'll get back to you, once I speak to Juanita.''

"Better make it as soon as possible. Those guys are going to be curious that one of their number is missing. They'll be along right sudden to see what happened to him.''

"Check with me in the morning.''

"You got it, Pard.''

Tito pushed back the chair and stood up. There was no need spending a sleepless night wondering about what Juanita would say to his proposal. He lifted a hand of farewell, heard Darby wish him luck, then went out of the saloon.

As it turned out, Juanita had not yet gone to bed for

the night. Contrarily, when he rode into the yard, she came out of the house, as if she had been waiting for him.

"I thought you might already be asleep," he offered, climbing down from his horse.

"I didn't . . ." She seemed awkward and unsure of herself. "When you left, you didn't say if you were coming back."

He realized what that meant. Juanita was in a state of limbo, without direction, not knowing what to expect. His generous treatment of her and the kids could well have been his going away present. The conclusion was obvious: she feared he might have left town and deserted her.

Tito unsaddled his horse. There was a little grass on one side of the house, mostly weeds. It appeared the dried-up milk cow had grazed there on occasion, but it still offered a little fodder. He used his rope and tethered the animal for the night. When he finished, he discovered Juanita standing a few feet away, patiently awaiting his attention.

"You didn't have to come back," she murmured quietly. "No one will break up our family, now that I have your name."

Tito stood and looked down at her. Unlike the first time or two he had seen her, the girl's hair was clean and glistening from being brushed. She wore the dress he had bought for her, and even the new shoes. She was posed, as if for a portrait or to have her photograph taken.

"I didn't realize how pretty you are," he said.

Juanita's eyes widened with surprise. Tito, himself, was stunned that he had simply blurted out something like that without thinking. He backed up a step, as if shocked.

"That's a very nice thing to say." Juanita broke the inauspicious silence which followed. "I . . . I've never had a man pay me a compliment before."

"I'm sorry," Tito said, regaining his composure. "I had no right to say that."

"Because it isn't true?"

He felt she was baiting him with that question, so he avoided answering it. "I didn't come here to make small talk."

"So why did you come?"

"I'm leaving for Broken Spoke tomorrow."

She was unable to mask her immediate reaction; she was crestfallen. "I see."

"I thought you and the kids . . ." He swallowed, searching for the words to present the idea properly. "That is, I was wondering if . . ."

"If what?" her eyes searched his face. He could see her holding her breath.

"I've got a run-down shanty, not even as good as this one you're living in now. The place is rocks and dust, not worth a grain of salt. However, with a little work, it might support a family."

"Are you asking us to come with you?"

He decided the question had been put forth. "Yes."

Juanita took an impulsive step toward him, then stopped herself. "I told you before, you are under no obligation, Mr. Pacheco."

"Nor are you."

She didn't answer him. Instead, she came to him and slipped her arms around his waist. She rested her head against his chest. He was not altogether certain what the act meant, but did have the presence of mind to encircle her in his arms. They stood there for a few long seconds. Then she pushed lightly against him. He quickly allowed her to escape his embrace.

"We will be ready when you are," she said in an oddly husky voice. Then she turned around and ran into the house.

Tito stood there staring blankly after her. "Darby was right," he muttered to himself and scratched his head. "Women and men don't think alike."

Chapter Ten

Luke Mallory continued to look up the street, watching for the stage to arrive. Timony Fairbourn, to whom he was engaged, sighed deeply. It caused him to turn his attention back to her.

"What exactly did Tito say in his wire?" she asked.

"I told you everything I know about this. The telegraph message said to meet him with a wagon. He is bringing a family to live on his homestead."

"You think he is going to hire someone to run the farm for him?"

"What can he raise on that hundred and sixty acres of rocks and hills? Other than having access to water, his claim was filled on an even worse piece of land than mine. Most of Wyoming wasn't meant for farming."

"I don't understand this, Luke. Tito takes a new job with Wells Fargo, finding and mapping routes for the stage lines in parts of Wyoming, Colorado, and Nebraska. Next thing we hear, he is sending you a wire from a town in Kansas. How did he end up in Kansas?"

"It is a little odd."

"Didn't Tito once tell you that he had only the two

cousins working up at Fielding's ranch, that he didn't have any other family in the country?''

''As I recall.''

''Then what about this family he is bringing to Broken Spoke?''

''I don't know any more than you. Maybe it's a family of sharecroppers.''

Timony took a sip of lemonade. At mid-morning, they were the only customers in the Ace High Saloon. Being both the café and saloon in Broken Spoke, there was no liquor served before three in the afternoon. There was the aroma of something being cooked in the kitchen. That would be Lee Chan preparing food for his noon offering. Cartwell Devine, the owner, was not working at the establishment. Instead, the one watching the place was Amber Ingersol, a young woman, who lived a mile or so out of town.

''The stage is late,'' Timony remarked after a few moments. ''When you were working for Wells Fargo, I used to come in and wait for the letters you never sent.''

A warning bell rang in Luke's head. ''I was a louse back then,'' he said quickly. ''I can't imagine why I ever thought a job was as important as being with you.''

''I can tell you how many ceiling beams are in this room,'' she went on. ''I counted the cracks in the floor, gave names to the two spiders who lived in the rafters, and watched Jack Cole's wretched cat lay around all morning like a discarded boot.''

''Don't start me on his cat, Harlot,'' Luke replied. ''If ever you needed proof that I was in love with you, sharing the jail cell with that mangy critter, just so I could remain in Broken Spoke, ought to be testimony enough.''

"How cold," she teased. "Jack says Harlot really loves you.''

"The selfish critter only wanted me for my ability to scratch her tummy or for rubbing against my leg. There never was any loyalty about her affection. I happen to know she is willing to throw herself at the feet of any man who comes around.''

Timony smiled. "Funny that she isn't attracted to women in the same way.''

Luke was on the verge of saying something about Nature, but the stage came rumbling up the street. He quickly rose to his feet and tossed a coin on the table. Timony was at his side, as they both went out the door of the saloon.

The man handling the reins was new to Luke, and so was the passenger sitting at his side. The stage came to a stop a few feet up the street and the driver put on the brake. He put down the reins as the other man climbed down. The two of them began unloading a pile of suitcases and bags from the top of the stage.

When the door opened, Tito was the first one to exit.

"Hey there, fella!" Luke called to him, "you get lost or something?''

A smile spread over Tito's face. "I guess you must have gotten my telegraph message.''

"Yeah, what's this about a fam. . . .'' Luke began. He lost the power to speak, as the others began to file out behind Tito. There came a pretty young lady, who stepped quickly over to stand with Tito, then a boy of maybe sixteen, a second boy who looked a year or two younger, a girl, another boy with a baby in his

GET 4 FREE BOOKS!

You can have the best Westerns delivered to your door for less than what you'd pay in a bookstore or online. Sign up for one of our book clubs today, and we'll send you **4 FREE* BOOKS**, worth $23.96, just for trying it out...**with no obligation to buy, ever!**

Authors include classic writers such as
LOUIS L'AMOUR, MAX BRAND, ZANE GREY
and more; PLUS new authors such as
COTTON SMITH, TIM CHAMPLIN, JOHNNY D. BOGGS
and others.

As a book club member you also receive the following special benefits:
- **30% OFF all orders through our website & telecenter!**
- **Exclusive access to special discounts!**
- **Convenient home delivery and 10 days to return any books you don't want to keep.**

There is no minimum number of books to buy,
and you may cancel membership at any time.
See back to sign up!

*Please include $2.00 for shipping and handling.

YES! ☐

Sign me up for the Leisure Western Book Club
and send my FOUR FREE BOOKS! If I choose to stay
in the club, I will pay only $14.00* each month,
a savings of $9.96!

NAME: _____

ADDRESS: _____

_____

TELEPHONE: _____

E-MAIL: _____

☐ **I WANT TO PAY BY CREDIT CARD.**

☐ VISA   ☐ MasterCard.   ☐ DISCOVER

ACCOUNT #: _____

EXPIRATION DATE: _____

SIGNATURE: _____

Send this card along with $2.00 shipping & handling to:

**Leisure Western Book Club
20 Academy Street
Norwalk, CT 06850-4032**

Or fax (must include credit card information!) to: 610.995.9274.
You can also sign up online at www.dorchesterpub.com.

*Plus $2.00 for shipping. Offer open to residents of the U.S. and Canada only.
Canadian residents please call 1.800.481.9191 for pricing information.

If under 18, a parent or guardian must sign. Terms, prices and conditions subject to change. Subscription subject
to acceptance. Dorchester Publishing reserves the right to reject any order or cancel any subscription.

JOIN NOW!

arms, and another girl of about six. Like a flock of sheep, they all gathered around Tito.

"Uh, meet the family, Luke," Tito said hesitantly.

"The family?"

"Yes, my new family."

Luke was too dumbfounded to speak. Timony, on the other hand, pulled him forward by the arm to meet the small tribe.

"You've been busy," she said. "Are these kids from a secret past or something?"

"They are my brothers and sisters, madam," the young lady spoke up with the reply. "My husband inherited them when he married me."

Now Timony was at a loss for words too. Luke and she exchanged looks, but neither could get their mental faculties working.

Bunion, the old gent who ran the livery, was there to greet the stage and help with the change of horses. He overheard the last of the conversation and hurried over to pump Tito's hand.

"By gum!" he said, possibly smiling under his thickly whiskered face. "You got yourself a whole passel of kids there, Pacheco. And this one here"— he put his eyes on the girl at his side—"she's about as cute as a bug's ear. Yes sir, she's a beauty." He paused to peek at the baby. "And a little tyke that ain't knee-high to a toadstool too. Well, don't this beat all."

"This is Juanita." Tito introduced the young lady first, then continued with the group. "And Pablo, Ricky, Ruben, Gena, Maria, and the baby is Inez."

"And I'm Darby," the blocky built youth, who had finished stacking the baggage from atop the stage, offered, moving in to shake hands with both Bunion and Luke. "Tito and I have been doing some traveling together."

"Mallory, Darby, and I need to speak to you about something important."

Luke recognized the clandestine expression on Tito's face. He rotated toward Timony. "Say, darlin', why don't you take the new arrivals inside and have Amber get them all some lemonade. I'll bet they are a thirsty lot from the stage ride up from Rimrock."

Timony understood and offered a quick smile at the family. "Mrs. Pacheco, won't you come with me? It only looks like a saloon. Actually, it's the only café in town too."

The girl hesitated, waiting for Tito to give his nod of approval. "Go ahead, Juanita. I'll put the family belongings in the wagon and be ready to leave in a few minutes."

As soon as the clan filed away with Timony, Tito faced Luke. He raised his hand to stop the flow of questions. "I'll explain some of this later, Mallory. Darby and I have a problem. I suspect it is something that will follow us to Broken Spoke."

"What kind of problem?"

Between Darby and Tito, the two illustrated what had taken place with Saul Puggot, the finding of Hermando Lopez's body, then the subsequent shoot-out with the unknown killer in Ivory Flats. When they finished, Luke had a general idea of the danger of the situation.

"You've been a busy man," Bunion said, having eavesdropped the whole time. "Any idea how many men this Puggot guy rides with?"

"I've heard up to a dozen at times," Darby answered. "I doubt he'll come looking with that many men, but it is a possibility."

"What are you going to do, Tito?"

"I need a place for the family. This is about the only home I've ever had."

"You don't expect to farm that pile of rocks?" Bunion asked.

"I thought I might get a milk cow or two, some chickens, and a few pigs. There's a little decent bottom ground down toward the stream, where we can have a garden and maybe raise a little feed for the animals. As long as I'm working for Wells Fargo, I ought to be able to keep food on the table and a roof over our heads."

"You know we'll lend a hand," Luke told him. "But what about this band of killers? You don't want those kids mixed up in a war."

"I don't have a lot of choices, Mallory. If Puggot comes gunning, I'll take him on as far away from town or my place as I can. I don't expect anyone else to fight my battles."

"You mean *we'll* take him on," Darby corrected. "You got into this fix because you saved my life. I ain't forgetting it."

"Count me in too, Tito," Luke added. "I owe you my life twice over."

"I'll throw in with you boys," Bunion offered. "Everyone in Broken Spoke owes you big time, Tito. Trouble comes looking, we'll send them fellers packing right sudden."

"We didn't leave much of a trail to follow," Tito

explained. "Met up with a guy on the train who said he knew you, Mallory—man named Deacon?"

Luke grinned. "Private story between him and me."

"He said he would pass the word to the others on board to forget we had ever been on the train. The Wells Fargo people also promised to keep quiet about when and where we took the stage. There's a chance those fellows will give up and go home."

"But we ain't going to count on it," Darby put in.

"Where did you leave your horses?"

"Rimrock. I'll take the stage back when I get settled and can start working again."

"I sold my nag," Darby added. "Needed a few dollars to hold me over. Anyone looking for help around here?"

Luke thought for a moment. "Winter is coming on, so most places cut back on their help. We can check around. Ought to be something you can do till spring. Where you going to stay?"

"I'll stick around town for a few days," Darby answered.

"I can maybe give him work for a week or so," Bunion proposed. "I've got to bring in some winter feed and replace a section of corral fence. That ought to hold him until one of the ranchers gets back to us."

"Sounds good," Tito said. "Thanks, Bunion."

Darby picked up a single bag. "Where should I stow my gear?"

"Take it over to the barn. You can bunk in the loft, unless it turns off real cold."

"No rooming house here in town?"

"Only a cell at Cole's place, and you have to share

it with an affectionate and rather aggressive, love-starved cat.''

''The loft sounds fine,'' Darby said. ''I don't care much for cats.''

With a rough idea of what lay ahead, Luke and Tito loaded up the few belongings of the Lopez family. Luke waited for an explanation, but Tito did not make the offer. As he put the last bag into the wagon, he could not hold back his curiosity.

''You going to tell me how you ended up married, with a whole family, or do I have to get rough and force it out of you?''

Tito displayed a sheepish grin. It was an expression that Luke had never seen on the man's face before, almost as if he was bashful to clarify what had taken place.

''It's a complicated story, Mallory.''

''I've been known to sort out a puzzle or two. Was Bunion right? Is this family from a secret past or something? I mean, you only said you picked them up after telling them about the death of their father.''

''Yeah, well, that's most of it. I never met any of them before I rode into Ivory Flats.''

''What about the wedding?''

''Juanita's my wife, legal and all.''

''Fast romance, Tito. I didn't know you were such a ladies' man.''

''It wasn't like that.'' He shrugged his shoulders. ''Do we have to do this right here and now?''

''Once I drop you and your new family off, Timony is going to grill me like a steak over hot coals. I'm looking out for my own self-preservation here. She'll want an explanation.''

"I told you, one of Puggot's men followed us. He braced me on the street in Ivory Flats and I killed him." He took a breath, as if trying to sort out the next words. "What happened next was about the strangest thing I've ever been a part of. I'm hauled off to a hearing and I'm about to be sentenced to two years in prison. Then Juanita walks up to the judge and tells him I'm the father and she's the mother of her baby sister. Instead of tossing me in prison, he tells me I'm married to her."

"Talk about your shotgun wedding."

"Yeah, you could call it that."

"So why stick with the ruse? You could have gotten the marriage annulled by any other judge in the country."

"I suppose."

"You suppose? You don't think that girl would have lied under oath?"

"No, she's not the type."

"Then once you pointed out to a judge that the baby was her sister and not her child, it would have been over."

"You're right."

"So, why continue the game?"

Tito sighed. "I've been a loner all of my life, Mallory. I've wandered from Mexico all across the Southwest looking for a home. When my cousins sent for me, it wasn't to become a member of their family, but only to prevent the cattlemen from running off Fielding's sheep. I've lived by my gun and wits while blowing around like a tumbleweed in a strong wind. Even when I joined your fight, it wasn't so that I could have a home of my own.

"Juanita and the others need me to keep their family together. If I hadn't married her, the kids would have been given away like a litter of unwanted puppies. Some might have never seen their brothers or sisters ever again."

"It's a noble cause, Tito," Luke said. "But what about you being married to Juanita? Is that what you really want?"

He paused, as if trying to decide the answer. "I don't know."

"You mean you don't know how to work out of the marriage, or don't know if you want to?"

Tito gave his head a shake. "She's only doing this to keep her family together, Mallory. I don't know how she really feels about me. What if she up and wants to see other men or something? What if she wants out of the deal? Where does that leave me?"

"You're afraid she'll dump you once they are settled?"

I don't know. I mean, she's mature in her thinking, Mallory, but she won't be nineteen for another month. How much does a girl change as she turns into a woman?"

"I don't know that their feelings change, Tito. If she's drawn to you, I reckon she won't even look at other guys."

"You know I'm going to turn thirty on my next birthday. I'm no kid anymore."

"Ten years isn't that much difference, not if you love each other."

Tito laughed. "Listen to us, Mallory! How could a woman ever love me? I've been a nomad gunman all my life. I've had to kill several times since the war in

Mexico. What is there to offer a woman and a bunch of kids?''

''Your past is only part of who you are, Tito. You have friends here, a home—such as it is—and you work for Wells Fargo. You're not a nomad gunman anymore, you're a respected citizen of Broken Spoke.''

''Let's get a move on, Mallory,'' Tito changed the subject after a moment. ''I've got to figure a way to house all of the kids in the shack those Irish settlers built. I haven't stayed there but a few times myself.''

''Once we get you settled, I'll fill a couple water barrels for you and bring them over. What about food?''

''Juanita can pick up a few things before we leave town. We'll get by with the fireplace until I can get us one of those cast-iron stoves from Cheyenne. I think I have enough pots and pans for cooking, but we'll need more plates, more stools, a decent chair or two, that sort of thing.''

''There's a cooking and heating stove already in town, over at the store. I ordered it for my place. You're welcome to take it. I can have another brought in before I'm ready to put it at my house. If you need a hand, you know you can count on me.''

''Thanks, Mallory. You're a big part of the reason I brought the family here. If something should happen to me, I expect you'll see them get by.''

''Nothing better happen to you, Tito. I sure wouldn't want the chore of adopting a family that size. You're the one who took on the job of raising that brood when you married Juanita. Volunteer or not, I expect you to stick around and finish what you got yourself into.''

"Let's join the others,'' Tito said. "I want to get home before dark. Somehow, I've got to figure out where to put everyone.''

"You've got one small shack for so many. Maybe you ought to send the two older boys over to my place.''

"Thanks, but we'll get by. The shanty they were staying in wasn't a whole lot bigger than mine.''

"Whatever you say, Tito,'' Luke said with a grin. "After all, they're your wife and kids.''

Tito grinned in return. "Yeah, they are at that.''

Chapter Eleven

Like many bullies, Vince Reel was not a brave man. He enjoyed wearing a badge for the power it gave him, but when faced with someone like Baxter Puggot and his boys, he was eager to comply with any of the man's wishes and answered every question put to him.

"This guy,"—Baxter grated each word—"you say he was working for Wells Fargo?"

"Came out at the trial. He said he was on their payroll. I don't know what his job was. Like I said, he took the Lopez family and left town. The other guy, Darby, he went with them."

"By stage?"

"No, they got a wagon here in town."

"And nobody knows where he was headed?"

"Toward Denver, but that's all I know."

Baxter stood with his hands on his hips, sulking, glowering at the floor, wondering what to do next. Marx tapped him on the shoulder.

"I've got a friend who works for Wells Fargo. I'll bet he can tell us about this fast gun."

Trapper came up to them and spoke in a hushed voice. "The deputy told it straight. They went west. A fellow at the edge of town saw them leave in a wagon, two guys and a passel of kids."

"Kids?" Baxter whirled back on Vince. "What kids?"

"Didn't I mention it?" He uttered a nervous laugh. "Yeah, the judge hitched that Pacheco fellow to a little señorita in the Lopez family. Stuck him with the whole lot. There was the girl and six kids, they all left with him and the other cowboy."

"That sure doesn't sound like the actions of a gunfighter, Bax," Nolen said. "What kind of man are we after? He up and marries some girl and takes on a whole family to raise."

"Probably some scheme he thought up," Trapper suggested. "Who is going to be looking for a family man?"

"It's going to backfire on him," Baxter said. "We won't have any trouble following a herd like that. They'll leave a trail a blind man could follow."

"So we head for Denver?"

Nolen put his hands on his hips, a worried frown on his face. "Denver is a fair-sized town, Bax. Plus, they've got a good many lawmen. If they go into hiding there, we'll have one tough time rooting them out."

"You have a better idea?"

"I'm only concerned that we don't end up in jail."

"We don't know the Mexican and his pal are going to set up camp in Denver," Marx put in. "Could be a trick of some kind. Maybe they are figuring we either won't follow them into a place like that, or else we'll lose them altogether."

"We need to find out where that cuss is going," Baxter said.

"Let me contact the guy at Wells Fargo," Mark

offered. "I know a few things about him that he wouldn't want the brass of the company to learn. Once we get a line on where this guy hangs his hat, we'll darn well track him down."

"All right, Marx." Baxter agreed to the idea. "You send off the wire and we'll get a room and spend the night here. See the horses get feed and a ration of oats. They need a rest."

Marx gave a nod. They could all use a little rest.

Amber Ingersol was thrilled to discover the package had arrived. She thanked Mrs. Devine, who was responsible for the mail delivery, tucked the box under her arm, and out the door she went.

"You'll have to show it to me this Sunday," Mrs. Devine called after her. "Be sure to wear it to the meeting."

Amber looked over her shoulder and answered, "I will!" However, as she was in such a hurry, she was not watching her step. By the time she discovered someone bending over on the walk, removing his spurs, it was too late to stop. She plowed right into him.

The force of the contact knocked the man right off the porch, sprawling onto his hands and knees. He lost his hat and one of the spurs flew from his hand, sailing over to strike a horse at the rail. The horse jumped forward, then kicked at the horse next to it. That horse jerked back from the hitching post and came loose. It backed into the water trough and shied away like it had seen a ghost. Before the man could retrieve his hat, the spooked horse planted one large hoof right in the middle of it.

The young man jumped up and caught hold of the horse. He secured it once more to the hitching rack, then recovered his spur and the flattened hat. Red-faced, with anger leaping from his eyes, he looked around to see who had sent him flying into the street. When he discovered the culprit was Amber, he instantly swallowed the anger.

"I'm truly sorry," she apologized as sweetly as possible. "I'm afraid I wasn't looking where I was going."

The man punched his hat, popping it back into shape, and lit up with a wide smile. "No harm done, ma'am." His voice was silky smooth. "It was my own fault for setting up in front of the door."

"I ain't seen you around before."

"No, ma'am, I came in with Tito Pacheco. The name's Driscoll Evanrude Shaughnessy, but everyone calls me Darby."

"Saves a lot of breath," she returned.

"Yes, ma'am, I was sixteen before I could spell my own name."

She giggled appropriately at his humor. "I'm Amber Ingersol. We have a farm northwest of town a bit."

"A real pleasure, Miss Amber. Can I offer to help with the package?"

"It ain't so heavy as it looks," she replied. Then, with a smile, she added, "But it would be a help if you could lift the canvas on my wagon, so's I can put it in the back. I'd like to protect it from the dust or if it should decide to rain."

Darby hurried to the waiting wagon and lifted a corner of the tarp. "It does look as if it might give us a shower this afternoon."

Amber slipped the package into the bed of the wagon and stepped back. Darby carefully secured the corner to a tie-down anchor. He pivoted to face her when he had finished and gave her another fleeting appraisal.

"Do you have some more shopping to do, or can I give you a helping hand up?"

"Thank you, I'm sure . . ."

"Miss Amber?" A familiar voice spoke up. The two of them rotated around and Amber spied Cully Deeks on the walk.

"Why, Mr. Deeks! What are you doing in town today?"

Cully put a hard stare on Darby. "Who's the little clown?"

Darby's chest puffed up. "Who you calling a little clown, Slim?"

Cully was a head taller than Darby, but not as stoutly built. He moved within a step to use his height to force the other man to look up at him.

"I seen you doing somersaults—figured it was to entertain the lady."

Darby displayed a cocky grin. "Well, Slim, I'd sure as shooting do somersaults to entertain someone as purty as her."

"You're crossing onto my property, sonny. I ain't real obliging about sharing the same pasture as you."

"Cully Deeks!" Amber snapped at him. "What do you mean, calling me your property? I'm not some horse or cow to have a brand set on my hip!"

Darby reached out and gave Cully a push. "See! You don't own the lady."

Cully backed up from the shove and pushed right back. Darby caught his balance and started swinging.

Amber jumped out of the way as the two exchanged a half-dozen punches. Then Darby grabbed onto Cully and both went down in a tangle of arms and legs. Before either could gain the advantage, Jack Cole came hobbling up the street. He waded in close enough to use his cane.

"Stop it, you dad-blamed knotheads!" he yelled. He began swatting them both about the head and arms with the walking stick. "You stop it right now!"

The words didn't carry near the authority or effect of being smacked smartly across the back of the head with his cane. Both men covered up from the punishment and broke different directions to escape the merciless beating.

"What's gotten into you, Deeks?" Cole snapped the question. "You ain't no ram what has to go butting heads over the first ewe that comes along."

"He started it," Cully replied, rubbing a tender spot on the back of his neck. "He pushed me first."

"I ain't the one who started calling names," Darby shot back.

Cole opened his mouth, as if to speak, then shut it tightly. Instead of continuing to scold the two men, he rotated about to look at Amber.

"Were you about to leave, Miss Ingersol?"

"Yes, Mr. Cole."

"No offense intended, but would you mind making some haste?" He gave a firm shake of his head. "I'm afraid these boys don't know proper behavior around a lady.''

Amber colored noticeably and she hurried to get up onto the wagon. Without a word or backward glance, she released the brake and struck the reins against the back of the team. As the dust was lifted by the wheels of her departing rig, Cole turned his attention back to the two men.

"Do I need to lock you boys up, or are you through with this foolishness?"

Cully dusted himself off and straightened his hat. The fire had left his eyes. "I reckon we can get along, Marshal. Just a misunderstanding, that's all."

"How about you, bub?" Cole diverted his gaze to Darby.

"Yeah, no hard feelings on my part, sir. We was just feeling our oats."

"Shake hands then."

Darby hesitated, but Cully finally stuck out his hand. "Sorry I called you a clown."

"Yeah," Darby replied, accepting the offering. "Well, I suppose it did look like I was doing a tumbling act for the lady." He grinned. "She kind of blindsided me, coming out the door the way she done."

"That's a mite careless, bending over in front of a door," Cully said. "Lucky for you that you didn't get stepped on by one of the horses."

Darby laughed. "Might say that I'll use enough hindsight next time to not camp in front of an entranceway."

Cully laughed. "You come in with Tito?"

"That's right."

"How about I buy you a drink. You can explain to me how he ended up married and the father of six kids."

"It's a story, all right."

"You boys mind if I tag along?" Cole asked. "Bunion tried to explain what transpired, but he's about as clear as a bowl of split-pea soup. I ain't been able to sort out all the details yet myself."

"You're welcome only if you want to do the buying of the drinks," Cully said. "I've got a welt the size of a silver dollar on the back of my skull from that cane of yours."

"He about knocked me senseless too," Darby agreed.

"All right, all right!" Cole snapped. "I didn't know you boys was such babies!"

"I'd like a chance to rap you a couple times with that stick," Cully returned. "Give us a chance to see how big a baby you are."

Cole grinned. "You ought to be thanking me, instead of griping. If I hadn't stopped you boys, one of you might have gotten hurt."

Cully gingerly fingered the lump. "Yeah, remind me to thank you when this here welt stops hurting."

Chapter Twelve

As the team pulled the wagon along the dusty road, Amber was filled with odd emotions. There was something incredibly stimulating about what had happened at the store. It was a foreign sensation, to think of as being sought after, but it was also pleasurable. She had been one of the boys all of her life. In reality, she felt she could physically have held her own against either Darby or Cully Deeks. However, this experience was something completely new.

When considering that either man might have been hurt during the encounter caused a very bad taste in her mouth. She had never enjoyed watching men fight. The punching and bleeding, the sight of someone being hurt, it was not something she relished. Her inner excitement was due to the reason behind the altercation, the fact that the two men were fighting over her! It stirred up emotions that had never come to the surface before.

Amber considered the night she had gone to the dance with Cully. He had been a perfect gentleman, holding her chair, catering the drinks from the punch bowl, addressing her with the utmost respect. Surprisingly, she discovered it to be very satisfying to have a man—or men—make a fuss over her.

She let the team plod at a slower pace than usual, inviting the thoughts to linger in her mind. The full impact of her having developed into womanhood was not a facet she had explored until their arrival in Broken Spoke. She had always hidden her feminine assets by way of bulky clothes and unflattering, cumbersome dresses. Since Cully had shown such an immediate interest, she had been inclined to dress more like a girl. There could be no denying the results. Men of all ages took notice of a young lady decked out in proper clothing.

A wrinkle furrowed her brow. She had drawn attention whenever she dressed in hand-me-downs from her brothers, but it was not the same thing. There was a definite distinction between being a curious spectacle and being admired and flirted with. She was quickly learning to enjoy the latter.

She was a mile from home when she caught sight of her brother. He was about a hundred yards off of the road, his rifle in the crook of his arm and a couple rabbits hooked onto his belt. He waved her down and she stopped the team to wait for him to reach the beaten trail.

"Hey, Sis! Good timing. I was just about to head back to the house."

"I see you got a couple rabbits for supper," she commented as he climbed up onto the wagon and sat down next to her.

"Could have knocked over another jack, but you know that meat is too stringy and tough. These cottontails are . . ."

Amber started the team moving again. It wasn't until she realized that Donny had stopped in midsentence that she looked at him. He had a curious expression on his face.

"What?" she asked.

"You've got on one of those new dresses Ray bought you."

"So?"

"And you're wearing your hair down. I thought you hated the way the dust and wind damaged your hair."

"There are clouds today and not much of a breeze."

He leaned over and sniffed. "By gum! You're even wearing some of that there fancy-smelling toilet water, the perfume stuff."

"What's the idea, Donny, is it pick-on-Amber day or something? Why shouldn't I dress up and try to look like a proper lady? And does it matter if I put on a little sweet-smelling stuff? Can't I look like a girl if I want to?"

"Whoa! I didn't mean nothing. I was only making conversation."

"We have to live with the people of Broken Spoke. You remember what Ma said about us all trying to make a good impression on them."

He studied her for a moment, then rubbed his chin thoughtfully. "Now that I reflect on it, you been wearing nothing but your work dresses ever since you went to the dance last month. Do that mean you don't like men's duds no more?"

"It don't mean nothing. Besides, I have to wear a dress when I work at the Ace High. Mr. Devine has done said so."

"You didn't work today."

"No, but I had to go into town and get some things for Ma."

Donny grinned. "I think maybe you figured to run into that Deeks fella in town. That's why you went to the trouble to get all prettied up."

"And maybe I'm only learning to enjoy being a woman. Is there something wrong with that?"

"Not a bit."

"And anyway, I've done noticed that men treat me a whole lot different when I'm wearing a dress."

Donny raised his brows. "How's that?"

"You know, they open doors, ask to help me carry things, and fuss over me." She had to smile at the thought. "It's kind of sweet."

"Figured as much."

"Figured what?"

"That you was turning into a girl. Next thing you know, there is going to be guys fighting to hold your hand or something."

"That's ridiculous."

"Maybe not." He lifted his shoulders in a shrug. "You're my sister, so's I don't guess I'm the right one to be judging, but I 'spect you're not exactly the cull of the herd. I mean, all made up like you are, I'd say there are a few young bucks out there who would lock horns to come courting."

She giggled.

"What's so funny?" Don asked. "I was being straight with you."

"It's your choice of words, Donny. It so happens I've already had two men fighting over me today."

"You don't say!"

"It wasn't a big fracas, 'cause the old marshal, Mr. Cole, he took his walking cane to the both of them and broke it up."

"But they was fighting over you?" He narrowed his gaze. "Who was it?"

"Cully Deeks and a new man in town called Darby."

"Darby, that's an odd name—the guy Irish or something?"

"He might be, but he didn't have any accent."

"But he and Cully Deeks started mixing it up over you, huh? That's something."

"Like I said, it wasn't much of a fight. No one got hurt, 'cepting for getting waled on with Marshal Cole's cane."

Donny laughed. "Little sister, you have done graduated to womanhood."

"I'm glad neither of them was hurt."

"I'll bet you are! Wouldn't want to have a couple crippled guys or men with all their teeth missing chasing after you."

"Don't tell Ma about it. I don't want her thinking I was starting trouble."

"You didn't provoke them, did you?"

"No, of course not."

"Well, then you got no reason to be hiding the truth. All the same, you wouldn't want her hearing about this at church or something. You might ought to mention it in passing, just so she don't think you are keeping secrets."

"I suppose."

Don stuck the rifle under the wagon seat and took the reins from Amber's hands. "Allow me to do the driving, ma'am." He grinned. "A proper lady needs herself a suitable escort."

Amber laughed, but was assailed by another strange

sensation. She had the feeling that her years of competing with her brothers had come to an end. Never before had Donny treated her like a lady, not even in jest. It added another point in favor of her transition to becoming a woman. She decided the benefits might even offset the agony of corsets and petticoats.

Tito blinked at a swirl of dust. "Wind coming up," he said to Luke. "Winter is only a few weeks away. We could get a cold spell any time."

"I think we'll make it. We only have a couple days' work to finish the addition." Luke glanced at the darkening sky. There were a few clouds, but the storm had passed by without any rain. "I reckon we better call it a night."

"I appreciate you lending me the material to add on to the house, Mallory. I know you were going to use this lumber for your own house."

"I've got time to get more, providing we don't get an early winter. You are the one in dire need. It's got to be as crowded in that shanty as the saloon on payday."

"I'm glad Cartwell Devine and Bunion helped me get the cooking stove out here. That makes it a little easier on Juanita."

"Takes up about half the space in the house though. I didn't realize just how huge those cook stoves could be."

"I'm surprised Juanita can find a place for all of the kids to sleep. She works sixteen hours a day and never complains a bit."

"She's seems like quite a girl."

Tito was silent for a moment. Luke looked at him

and could see the man had something on his mind. After giving him a few seconds to speak, he asked, "What about the wedding vows you took? Have you made a decision yet?"

"About what?"

"About you possibly taking this marriage serious, as if you are legally hitched." He watched for his reaction. "Or are you still being a good Samaritan?"

"I don't know, Mallory. We haven't spoken about it since that day."

"You've had time to ponder on it some. How do you feel about the whole deal? You were duped into a pretense wedding and saddled with six kids. Don't tell me you haven't been giving some thought as to what you're going to do?"

"I told you before, Juanita needed my name, so she would be able to keep the family together. If I hadn't married her, there's a very good chance the kids would have been split up. There's no way she and the oldest boys could have supported so many children."

"Then you're serious about keeping this as a real marriage?"

"The judge said he would send an annulment after a few days. I haven't yet decided what I'll do if and when the paper shows up."

"How much leave did you take from Wells Fargo?"

"Only another week. I've got to take the stage back to Rimrock and pick up my horse in a couple days."

"And then?"

Tito shrugged. "I don't know."

"Okay, so you have the milk cow and chickens we bought from Tom Kensington, and John Fairbourn brought by a side of beef. With the supplies you picked up in town, I'd say the family can get by for a couple weeks.''

"We still need to dig a well. With the creek nearby, I doubt we'll have to go too deep, but it's quite a chore to go down to the creek and back to fill a barrel every couple days.''

"You know you're welcome to come over to my place for water. The windmill is working better than expected. It produces a lot more than I can use.''

"We have to cross the creek to get to you. Besides, when winter arrives, your windmill is likely going to be frozen solid for several weeks or even months at a time.''

"It might.''

Juanita appeared in the doorway to the house. "Tito,'' she said softly, as if embarrassed to call him by name, "I'll have supper ready in about ten minutes.''

"Okay. Set a place for Mallory here.''

"I have.''

Tito's eyes lingered after her, as she turned and went back into the house. He sighed and shook his head.

"I don't know how to proceed, Mallory.''

"Maybe you ought to try a little courting. You haven't forgotten how to do that, have you?''

"You don't understand. She tricked me into the marriage. She thinks I'm only being a decent guy and helping her keep her family together. Far as I know, she might figure I hold it against her for being deceived.''

"And do you?''

"No."

"Maybe you ought to tell her that."

Tito walked over to the horse trough and began to wash the dirt from his hands. Luke followed suit, waiting for him to continue.

"There's Puggot to worry about too, Mallory. He's going to come gunning for Darby and me. It concerns me that those gunmen might come out here looking for us."

"If they come to Broken Spoke, it'll be the worst mistake they could make."

"What if he rides in with a dozen hard-case gunmen? I'm not talking about cowboys or farmers, but bounty killers, men who make their living with guns. What chance will we have against those odds?"

"Preston Hytower brought in gunmen, when he tried to take over the valley. We beat him, we can beat Puggot."

"That was different. We were up against a half-dozen men, and they pretty much stayed within the boundaries of the law. These killers aren't going to recognize any law. Anyone standing in their way is going to get run over."

"Do you have another idea?"

"I think I ought to ride out and not look back. When Puggot comes, you send him after me. I'll find a place where I can take him on, far enough away that no one else will get hurt."

"You alone, against a dozen guns. That's no idea, it's ridiculous."

"It isn't!" Tito cried. "I don't want these kids getting hurt, and I don't want you and half of the people in town to get shot or killed! I'm trying to figure a way out so that no one else is involved.''

"No one else involved?'' Luke's right hand shot out and he grabbed Tito's arm. He put a hard stare on him. "Durn your hide, Pacheco! You don't have the right to say something like that to me!''

"What?''

"You saved my life more than once, you took a hand in my battles, and now you are telling me that I can't return the favor.'' He squeezed until Tito grimaced from the pain. "Don't you dare try and play this hand alone! I won't stand for it!''

"Yeah, but—''

"But nothing!'' Luke snapped. "Good people will always rally together in order to overcome the bad. You've been there when I needed you. Well, I'll be hanged if you don't let me and the other people in this valley stand by you. We'll deal with Puggot if he shows up. I don't care if he comes with an entire army. We'll deal with him—all of us!''

"You sound as if you've made up your mind.''

"That's right, so let's go see if your wife can cook.''

Tito smiled as Luke released his grip on his arm. "With the new stove in place, I'm for believing she can turn buzzard into fried chicken.''

"After eating my own cooking the past few weeks, I'll even try the buzzard.''

Chapter Thirteen

After dinner, Tito watched Luke ride off toward his own place, on the opposite side of the Dakota Creek. For a time, he remained standing in the dark. He wondered how many more nights he could enjoy the serenity of the evening. Puggot was certain to find out he worked for Wells Fargo—it had come out at his hearing in Ivory Flats. He would follow his trail back to Broken Spoke and come looking for him. There was no escaping the inevitable. It nagged at his conscience that he might have been better off to stay at Fallwood or Ivory Flats and face the man and his guns. The odds would not have been good, but he would not be risking the lives of his friends.

He thought of Luke, Bunion, Jack Cole, the farmers, and men like John Fairbourn, head of the Ranchers Association. They were all good, honest men. With the support of those men and their guns, he could beat Puggot.

But at what cost? he wondered. How many of them would be killed or wounded? He hated the idea of bringing them into a fight that wasn't their own.

"You can't keep sleeping outside." Juanita's voice shattered his own reflections. He had not heard her come out the door. "It's getting too cold at nights."

"We have the walls in place for the addition," he answered, still staring out into the darkness. "Tomorrow, with Luke and the boys helping, I think we'll finish the roof. The house is going to look like it was built by a couple drunk miners, but it should keep the snow off and shut out most of the wind."

The girl moved up to stand at his side. "You are a very good man, Tito."

He felt a warm flush rise into his cheeks. It was a curious sensation. Before he met Juanita, throughout his entire life, he could remember blushing only once or twice. But now, every time she was close to him, each time she would speak, he felt the heat rise like a wall of flame before his face.

"If something should happen to me, Mallory and the others will see that you keep the house and get by."

"Don't you dare say such a thing!"

His head swiveled around at the sharpness of her words. "It's a possibility we have to face."

She gave her head a negative shake. "No it isn't! Nothing is going to happen to you. I won't have you talking like that."

Tito stared at her. He was unable to see her clearly, for there was but a single candle showing from inside the cabin, and the door was scarcely ajar. All of the kids were down for the night, the three boys crowded into a makeshift bed on one side, the two girls on the other, with the baby asleep in her small cradle. Tito did not want to frighten the children, so he took Juanita's arm and the two of them walked a short distance from the house.

"Puggot and his men will come, Juanita," he said,

stopping after a short way. "I'm very good with a gun, but they are not the sort of men to play fair. We have to consider what might happen."

"I heard Luke talking to you." She ducked her head, as if ashamed of eavesdropping. "He said the entire valley would help you. This Puggot can't be so tough that he can beat everyone in Broken Spoke."

"I've heard words like those spoken before," he said. "People are often fearless and full of support, until they meet the face of the enemy. I was in a war with some of my own people in Mexico. Many times I heard the bragging of my comrades, how they would stand and fight for what we believed. In the end, a good many of them ran. Faced with certain death, a large share of strong, good-hearted men will flee for their lives. It isn't anything cowardly, it is human nature to want to survive."

"And what of the men like you, those who do not run in the face of certain death?" She looked up into his eyes. "I believe Mr. Mallory is that kind of man. There is also Darby and probably others here too."

"Except for Darby, this isn't their fight!"

"And is it really yours?" she asked, showing an impatience he had not seen before. "Did you ask to have to shoot Saul Puggot or that man in Ivory Flats? Did you go looking for a fight and end up killing those men?"

"No, but it won't matter to Baxter Puggot."

"Well, it matters to these people in Broken Spoke. They are your friends. I've heard them say how you have stood and fought with them before. They won't desert you."

"And what if I get a lot of them killed?"

"Do you really think they will blame you? I heard Mr. Mallory say you risked your life for them! Isn't this the same thing, they risking their lives for you?"

"I don't know."

"Tito." Juanita's voice was suddenly very soft. "I don't want anything to happen to you. You are the best man I have ever known in my life. Few men in this country would have taken on a family like mine, two near adults and five children. Had you given me a few dollars and ridden out of town, I would have been eternally grateful! You didn't have to stay with us."

Tito was now the one to duck his head. Although it was too dark to read the expression in the girl's face, he could feel her sincerity. He uttered a sigh and said, "I don't want you feeling indebted to me, Juanita."

"How can I not feel a debt to you?"

"I would rather you forget the circumstances of our—" he searched for the word—"our rather dubious union."

"Dubious?"

He wondered if she understood the word. "Juanita, I would like . . . I mean . . ."

"What, Tito?" The girl whispered his name. "What would you like?"

He gulped, unable to blurt out his feelings. "I'd like for this vendetta thing to be over," he muttered, caving in from the pressure he felt. "I hate putting all of you in danger."

She smiled. "Don't you worry about us. We'll get through this thing—together."

"But . . ."

"Come inside. It's getting late."

"It isn't so cold at nights yet. I can make a bed against one of the new walls. It's too crowded inside as it is."

"You can sleep next to the boys," she said with some authority. "I already made up a bed for you."

Tito had no choice but to follow after her. He cursed his own weakness. How could he tell her how he felt, when the fear inside him kept reminding him that this girl was too good for him? She was so young, so virtuous, so special. He knew she would not laugh in his face. She had too much tact, plus she did owe him a monumental favor. There was a good chance she would not resist, had he tried to kiss her.

But I don't want her to submit to me out of gratitude! he lamented inwardly. *I want her to feel passion and love for me! How do I do that? How can I ever know her true feelings?*

The meeting had been called without Tito's knowledge. Luke had decided not to put any pressure on anyone. If a man was to risk his life, he felt it ought to be of his own choosing.

Cartwell Devine took charge, calling the assembly to order. He looked around the room and determined they were all present. Of the ranchers, John and Billy Fairbourn were there, Henry Fielding, Cully Deeks, Big George, Von Gustin, Indian Joe, and Mont Hytower. For the farmers, Dexter Cline, Ray Ingersol, and Tom Kensington. Bunion and Jack Cole sat in for the townspeople.

"I believe everyone here knows the reason for this here meeting," Cartwell declared. "We have a pack of gunmen headed this way, a bad hombre named

Baxter Puggot and possibly as many as a dozen hard-case gunmen.''

"We've heard the story," Dexter said. "Tito shot Puggot's brother to save the life of young Darby, then killed a second one of Puggot's men over in Kansas."

"That's right."

"We going to shoot these men on sight?" Ray asked.

"No one knows what any of them look like," Bunion answered him. "You can't go popping away at every stranger who comes into town."

"I imagine they will make their presence known to us quick enough," Cartwell said. "I'd venture they will scout the town first and try to make certain Tito is here."

"What if he's gone?" Mont wanted to know. "I mean, Tito works for Wells Fargo. He is often gone for days or even weeks at a time. What happens if those fellows come looking while he is out of town?"

"Yeah, are we supposed to do all his fighting for him?" Von Gustin chirped.

"How do we watch out for that family he brung with him?" another question arose. There were suddenly more questions. Who was going to organize this fight? What were they supposed to do? How many killers were they talking about? Did anyone know what any of the men looked like?

"Hold on!" Cartwell raised his hands to silence the crowd. "Enough questions already! That's why we're having this here meeting."

"You been real quiet, Mallory," Dexter looked over at Luke. "What kind of plan do you have in mind?"

"Yeah," Mont agreed, "you are often an acting deputy for Marshal Cole. Have you two come up with any ideas?"

Jack Cole cleared his throat. "Actually, I was going to ask Luke to pin on a badge until this thing blows over. Maybe Indian Joe too."

Joe displayed no emotion, so Luke stood up to address the group. "I'll gladly wear a badge, but Joe is new here in Broken Spoke. He helped us find a kidnapped woman and bring some killers to justice, but he is his own man."

All eyes on the room turned to the Shoshone Indian. Joe glanced around the room, possibly wondering if these men would ever go to battle on his behalf. "I have never met Mr. Pacheco," he began. "I know a few of you here by your names or faces, but I doubt many of you would call me a friend."

"I would," Ray Ingersol said, "me and my brother too."

Luke took the floor again. "These men coming to Broken Spoke are the worst kind of manhunters, Joe. Tito said they have murdered a good many red and white fugitives in cold blood. They sound like the most ruthless bunch of killers in the country. No one is going to hold it against you if you were to decide not to join in on this fight."

"What I was going to say, white eyes—" he used the pet name he had given to Luke—"is that I was not altogether certain everyone would want me to be a part of this. I'm pretty much a stranger here. I've only been working for Mr. Hytower for a few weeks."

"And a fine hand he is too," Mont said in his behalf. "Most of you probably know I've made him my foreman. I'll tell you this much, I would trust him with my ranch, my money, or even my life.''

Luke had to smile as Joe showed a trace of embarrassment at such a testimony. He said, "If you would be willing to part with him for a short while, Mont, I could use Joe to pin on a badge till this is over.''

"It's like you said, Mallory, Joe's his own man. Whatever he wants to do, I'll pay his salary either way.''

The young man gave a slight nod of his head. He would join Luke in the fight.

''Maybe you ought to deputize me and my brother, too,'' Ray suggested. ''Those men ride into town and see we have a dozen marshals, they might think twice about starting something.''

''It's a thought, Ray, but I don't think we can count on forcing these guys to back down. Cole got a rundown on them by telegraph. Baxter usually has at least six men who ride with him, sometimes more. Cole, you want to tell us what you learned about these guys?''

''I sent a wire to several places, a fort or two, and a couple towns over where this fellow, Puggot, does most of his dirty work.'' Cole removed a piece of paper from his pocket and looked at it. ''Most of the time, he rides with five or six men. About all we have are the names of the usual guns who ride with him. They are Link Nolen, Trapper Collins, Vance Walters, a fellow named Chiggers, and Otto Marx. There are a few others that join him from time to time. The man Tito killed in Ivory Flats was Quint Avery, one of Puggot's regulars.''

"That ain't so bad," Bunion spoke up. "Only five or six men."

"He might bring more."

"Anyone have something to add?" Cartwell wanted to know.

"I'd as soon keep any fight away from my farm," Dexter spoke up. "I'll throw in with you boys, but I've got my wife, three girls, and a boy at home. I sure wouldn't want any stray bullets flying around my farm."

"Same here," Tom agreed. "We need to control where any confrontation takes place."

"Wouldn't want it out at Tito's place," John Fairbourn pointed out. "He's got six young'uns and his new bride at his house."

"Why didn't you invite Tito or Darby?" Billy asked.

"We don't want no one feeling they was pressured into this," Cole replied. "This is a free country and this is an open meeting. You are all men with a conscience and a mind of your own. No one has to join in this here fight what don't have the mind-set for it."

Fielding stood up, one of the oldest fellows in the room. He had been down sick for a number of weeks and was about as thin and frail as a man made of twigs. When he spoke, however, his voice showed he still had strength of will and determination.

"I, for one, owe a great deal to Tito," he said. "If not for him, you ranchers might never have allowed for me and my sheep to settle here in Broken Spoke. Trouble is, I don't have no fighting men. Not even Tito's cousins—they are sheepherders, not fighters.

We'll do what we can, but about the only good we would be in a gun battle is as targets for them killers.''

John was next to stand. "Speaking for myself, and not as the head of the Ranchers Association, my foreman, Token, Billy, and myself will stand with Tito.''

"Same with me and my brother too!'' Ray said. "This here is our home. Ain't no one going to ride in here and threaten one of our neighbors.''

"Count me in,'' Cully Deeks added.

One by one, all of the men in the room vowed to stand against Puggot's men. It was a sealing of comradeship, a union of men from several walks of life, even those who had fought one another in the past. All were united against a common foe.

Chapter Fourteen

Nolen stood before Baxter, steadfast, not giving an inch. He met the man's glare with a cool stare of his own.

"You going yella' on me, Nolen?" Baxter roared.

"I'm telling you, Bax, this won't be a walk around the maypole! Marx told us that Tito Pacheco has friends in Broken Spoke, one an ex–Wells Fargo teamster named Mallory. Story is, they've been through a few scrapes together and that means we're liable to end up riding against a whole army."

"I'm going to kill the two men responsible for Saul's death. I ain't asking no one to go with me."

"You know we're with you, Bax. What I'm saying is we need to approach this with some degree of caution. That Mexican downed Quint in a gunfight, and the deputy said Quint took him by surprise. He was sitting down when he beat Saul to the draw too. We have to consider him to be a holy terror with a gun."

"So?"

"The other teamster pal of his might also be good with a gun. Add the green cowboy to the pot and a few friends and we're outnumbered and maybe outgunned as well."

"What's your idea then, simply toss your backbone

to the wind and give up?" Baxter turned and spat onto the ground. "You know there ain't no way I'm quitting!"

"I'm only saying we might need to get a couple more men. We're already looking at three or four guns. If those guys have friends, we might be up against a dozen."

Baxter did some thinking. "I suppose you could be right on that count, Nolen. Any ideas on who can we get?"

"The Domino Kid is in Denver," Marx offered. "He usually has Chipper Haynes and the Swede with him. With those three along, we'd have a fair-sized army of our own."

"Domino is always for hire, if the price is right. I've got a thousand dollars with me. I'll bet it would be enough to get all three men. We'd have a bigger edge with them along."

"Picking them up shouldn't be a problem. We'd only need them for a few days, and last I heard, Domino was running a streak of bad luck. He and some of his pals have been riding shotgun for mine shipments for sixty dollars a month. I'll bet they jump at any kind of offer to make some real money."

"All right, we've got to catch the train in Denver anyway. Marx, you and Nolen send off a telegram and we'll try and meet up with Domino when we arrive."

The two men hurried off toward the telegraph office. Baxter watched them go. He had no doubts about Marx, the man was cold as a fish. Nolen, however, remained an unanswered question. He had been riding with him for over a year and he still didn't understand the man. He was the best handler of horseflesh he had ever known. He did the job given, so long as it was concerning the hunting and tracking of their prey. He packed the gear and did most of the cooking when they were running down fugitives, but when Bax stopped to think back, he couldn't recall Nolen ever shooting any of the men they had cornered or trapped. He was tough, but lacked the killer instinct. With a shake of his head, Baxter decided he would have to keep an eye on Nolen. It wouldn't do to have him influencing any of the others.

Walt wandered over to stand at his side. "Horses are watered and ready, Bax. We've got enough supplies for maybe a week."

"Shouldn't take us that long to flush out the quail we're hunting."

"Heard Nolen and Marx talking to you. We going to pick up the Domino Kid?"

"Seems like a good way to keep the advantage in any kind of fight. Nolen is scared the Mexican might have friends in Broken Spoke."

"I've never done much riding in Wyoming. It's mostly cattle country, ain't it?"

"There are a few farms around Broken Spoke, but they've got cattle and sheep too."

"And they all get along?"

"I heard about a fracas between the farmers and ranchers some time back, but they settled it with only a shooting or two."

"Think Nolen is right about the whole town throwing in against us?"

"With Domino and his two buddies, it won't matter. We'll have enough firepower to squash anything they throw against us."

"Have you got a plan of attack?"

"Once we get close, we'll send in a couple of the boys to look the place over and see what we're up against. I aim to see those two jaspers dying in their own blood, but it don't mean I intend to get any of us killed in the process."

"We could do the chore by ambush," Walt suggested. "A couple of rifles, a shot apiece, and the job is done."

"Only as a last resort. I want to look into the eyes of the cowboy and that Mexican. I want them to know they are going to die."

"I understand how you feel, Bax."

"Round up the boys. We've got a few miles to cover today."

He didn't speak again, but hurried off to get the others.

Baxter stared off in the direction of Wyoming, with no attempt to focus on anything in sight. He set his teeth, his thick jowls locked with his determination. Somewhere beyond the horizon was the man who had killed Saul. He was probably laughing and telling stories, thinking he had made a clean getaway. Who was going to mistake a man traveling with a half-dozen kids for some wandering gunman? It was the perfect way to hide—behind the youngsters.

"Yeah, well it ain't going to work." He hissed the words under his breath. "Enjoy yourself while you can, Tito Pacheco. Your days are numbered, and it's a mighty small number at that!"

Amber paused from her sewing as she saw a rider coming down the trail. Before he reached the yard, she set aside her needle and thread. "I'll be back in a minute," she called to her mother, who was in the midst of baking bread in the next room.

Mrs. Ingersol frowned appropriately. "Another cowboy coming to visit?"

"I won't be long." Amber avoided answering the question, quickly making her exit. She stopped to close the door and waited for Cully Deeks to pull up his horse. He removed his hat in a polite gesture.

"Good day, Miss Amber."

"Mr. Deeks." She offered him a smile. "I've been wondering when you'd stop by."

"I'd like to apologize for the way I acted in town. It was wrong of me to talk about you as if you were property."

"Yes, it certainly was."

He slid to the ground, his hat still in one hand, head ducked slightly. "I was being impetuous," he said, sounding rather proud of the word. "I expect a man shouldn't be impetuous to the point where he starts saying things he shouldn't."

"I agree."

"As far as that Darby fellow goes, he isn't such a bad guy. We had a drink later on and shook hands. I wanted you to know that I was sorry for starting trouble."

"Mr. Darby was being the perfect gentleman. There was no need to cause such a fuss."

"I know you're right, Miss Amber. I just got hot, when I seen you smiling at him."

She felt a flutter inside. "Why should you be upset at such a thing?"

He lifted his head and stared deep into her eyes. "I

expect you know why, Miss Amber. I've taken a real shine to you. Them feelings is what caused me to act impetuous.''

"Sounds more like jealousy to me."

"I expect you could call it that too."

"You can't be getting jealous and all over me speaking to another man, Mr. Deeks. I only went to one dance with you. We ain't been on no picnics or done any courting since. I ain't made any promises to you."

"I know, and I apologize again." He twisted the hat between his hands. "There is something else I've been thinking on, Miss Amber."

"And what is that?"

"Well, I'd admire to solicit your favor, on a regular-type basis, that is."

"Ma already allowed you could come courting."

Cully continued to turn the hat nervously. "Yes, ma'am."

"But you don't have no right to stake claim to me as if I was property," she scolded him. "That won't happen until I've got a ring on my finger and have promised to have and hold to one man. You understand?"

"Yes, ma'am."

"So, that's settled."

"I expect so."

"And quit calling me ma'am—I ain't your mother."

"No, Miss Amber." He grinned. "You're nothing like my mother."

She smiled at how easily it was to tame a full-grown man. All of her life she had wasted time doing physical and verbal battle with her brothers. What a waste of energy, when it took only the proper demeanor, a little feminine innovation, and acting the part of a lady to get her way.

"Did you come to ask me to the dance Saturday night?"

"There's another part of the reason I come to see you. I can't be at the dance." He uttered a groaned. "I drew straws with Luke, John, and Billy for the watch and lost. I have to keep an eye out for those killers Saturday night."

Amber felt an immediate disappointment. "But I've got a new dress! It only arrived yesterday. That's why I was in town!"

"I'm right sorry, really I am."

"I won't be staying home, Mr. Deeks," she vowed. "I'll tell you that much right up front. I'm going to the dance, even if I have to ride in with my brothers. You know that means I'll likely be dancing with other men."

He looked sick at the thought. "Yes, ma'am."

"I don't want you starting any trouble because of it. You hear me?"

"Yes, Miss Amber, I won't cause no ruckus."

She simmered, able to tell how it hurt him to have her going to the dance without him. "Is there anything else you wanted to say?"

Cully was within arm's reach. That's what he used—his arm's reach—to pull her to him. Before Amber knew what he was up to, he kissed her flush on the mouth. When she didn't resist, he held her in such a position for a full three seconds!

Finally, he released her, stepped back, and turned

his head slightly, chin extended enough to make a good target.

"Slap me, if you've a mind to, Miss Amber," he offered, "but I really felt I had to do that."

"Let me guess," she gasped, slightly out of breath, "you was only being impetuous again."

He held the pose a moment longer, then, satisfied she was not going to slap him, he relaxed. "I guess I wanted to see if you'd allow me the privilege."

"One time only, Mr. Deeks," she warned. "If ever you try being so forward again, without my permission, I'll have my brothers pound you into bonemeal or I'll whoop you myself."

"I'll remember."

She flashed an impish simper. "I really didn't know you had so much courage—to dare and kiss me without asking first."

Cully backed up a step and put his hat on. "Around you, Miss Amber, there are a lot of things I do that are downright confusing to me too."

"I'll miss you at the dance."

He mounted his horse and looked down at her. "Not nearly so much as I'll miss being with you."

"Good day, Cully."

The use of his first name put a wide smile on his lips. "Good day, Miss Amber."

Chapter Fifteen

Luke located Joe out near the cattle. The Shoshone Indian was dressed like an ordinary cowboy, right down to his shinny spurs. He tipped back his straw hat and grinned at Luke's approach. "What brings you to our corner of the world, white eyes?"

Luke chuckled at his pet name. "I've gone back to work for Wells Fargo. Starting Monday, I take the stage run between Rimrock and Broken Spoke twice a week. It isn't much, but at least I'll have a little money coming in every month. No telling how long it will take for my rock farm to produce enough to support us."

"When you and Miss Fairbourn finally engage in marital bliss, isn't a third of her place going to be yours?"

"Not exactly. There are several hired hands, a foreman and his wife, plus John and Billy are still living on the ranch. Timony's share comes to about a hundred and fifty head of cattle. We'll leave them on the Fairbourn ranch to build the herd. She has something worked out with John as to the feeding and tending of the animals. When all is said and done, we won't make a lot of money there for some time to come."

"So much for marrying the daughter of a prosperous rancher," he said with a grunt. "Used to be, if a man married well—red or white—he was set for life."

"The reason I came looking for you, Joe," he said and sighed, "I've got a favor to ask."

"Let me guess, it has something to do with Tito Pacheco?"

Luke pulled a badge from his pocket. "As I'll be out of town for a day or two at a time, Cole and I thought you should wear a badge too."

"It'll make a pretty target for any of Puggot's men to shoot at," Joe said, "especially with me being an Indian too."

"I know we all agreed to help him against Baxter Puggot at the meeting. However, I want to give you a chance to step out of the fight. You're a new man here in Broken Spoke. You don't owe Tito or any of the rest of us anything."

"I gave my word, same as you. Being a red man, I believe my word is better than your own."

"Could be."

"So, are you adding something else to the story of Tito's sordid life, or do you simply enjoy hearing your own voice?"

"Puggot doesn't sound like the kind of man to give up a hunt. I reckon he is going to show up one day soon, probably with a dozen men at his side."

"I didn't sleep through the town meeting, white eyes. I know the odds."

"You don't have to be in this fight."

"Considering I am already in the fight, what else do you want from me?"

Luke did not hide his relief. "You're the best

tracker I've ever seen, and I reckon you have the stealth of a coyote.''

''If you're trying to impress me with flattery, you can stop. I won't go to the dance with you next Saturday night.'' He grinned. ''You're too tall for me.''

''I like to lead too.''

Joe chuckled, then grew serious. ''Any new information about these bounty killers? Do we know anything more about their background? Any descriptions on what they look like? Are they back-shooters or stand-up fighters?''

''We've no idea, other than they sound like the worst breed of men since the scalp hunters of days gone by. Only a bunch of hardened killers without conscience could shoot down so many men in cold blood.''

''You have to give them some credit. Their method of dealing with prisoners does keep the jails from filling up.''

''What I'd like is for you to keep an eye out for those fellows. I'd do it myself, but I've got the stage run now, and there is still a lot of work to be done on Tito's new home. Plus, I've got to finish up my own before my wedding date. I simply haven't got time to—''

Joe held up a hand. ''I'm working for Mr. Hytower. Did you check with him first?''

''I spoke to Mont before I came looking for you. He said the choice was yours.''

''And the work around the place?''

''He's going to hire Darby, the man who rode in with Tito. He is helping Bunion for a day or two, but then he'll be able to help with the work around here.

He can do whatever Mont needs done until we deal with these bounty hunters."

"All right, white eyes, I don't mind doing a little scouting around. Besides, Tito seems like a nice guy." With a grin, he added, "I figure he must be either a real upstanding guy or a complete idiot to take in seven kids."

"You'll need to be careful, Joe. Those killers wouldn't hesitate to shoot you on sight. You only need to get word to us as to how many there are and where they are at. After that, it'll be all of us in the valley against their small army."

"I'll keep a discreet distance."

"If you spot them, get word to any of us, John, Billy, Tito, or me. Soon as we know what we're up against, we'll devise a plan to take them on. I don't—"

Before he could finish, Joe pointed to an oncoming rider. "Looks like Big George's foreman."

"Yeah, Cully Deeks. I wonder what he's doing over this way."

Cully saw them and angled his steed through the brush until he reached the same clearing. He stopped his horse, hooked a leg over the pommel of his saddle, and pushed back his hat. "What's going on, gents? You both look real serious."

"Discussing our predicament, Deeks," Luke answered. "I was asking Joe here if he could keep an eye out for Puggot's gang."

"He can cover for me tomorrow night. I hate to miss the dance."

"We drew straws after the meeting, Deeks," Luke reminded him. "You lost."

"All right, all right, it was worth a shot."

"To keep watch twenty-four hours will take more than one man," Joe put in.

"There's a coincidence for you. Big George just gave me the go-ahead to do nothing but keep watch for them fellers. I figured you and I could work together on that, Injun Joe."

"I was about to suggest the same thing, Deeks."

"When they come, the logical approach would be by way of the main trail from Rimrock," Luke surmised. "Still, we can't take that chance. They could circle and come in from about any direction."

"They might ride right into town like they own it," Cully suggested. "You said these men were bounty hunters. The few I've met in that line of work are not exactly squeamish about throwing their weight around."

"Depends on what they've picked up," Joe said. "If they take time to learn something about Broken Spoke, they might be a trifle more cautious. We are at the disadvantage here, because we don't know how much information they have about us."

"What do you think, Luke?" Cully asked. "You got any ideas on how they might handle it?"

"If it were me, and I didn't have an informer in town, I would send a couple men to scout around first. I should think they would want to know the disposition of the land, how many guns they'll be up against, even where to locate Tito and Darby. My guess is, they will send a man or two ahead to survey the valley and estimate the odds against them."

"A good many people travel through Broken Spoke. How are we going to know who to look for?"

Luke grunted. "I reckon we'll have to be a little smarter than they are."

"Shouldn't be much of a challenge," Joe said, displaying a grin. "After all, they only have white men on their side, while the people of Broken Spoke have me."

Tito felt the difference, a coolness in Juanita's attitude. She put the meal on the table so all of the children could eat. Ricky and Pablo left the room first, returning to their chore of gathering wood and cow chips for the coming winter. Once the baby was fed and put down for her nap, Tito finally had a moment alone with Juanita.

"There's a dance in town tonight," he said easily. "How about you and I go with Luke and Timony?"

"I don't think so."

"We don't have to actually dance, if you don't want to. However, I was thinking it would give you a chance to meet some of the other people from around town."

When she looked directly at him, he felt as if he'd been jabbed with something sharp. Her eyes pierced into him like twin shards of ice.

"You don't have to pretend anymore, Tito. The paper arrived while you were over at Mr. Mallory's place. You are a free man again."

"What?" he was stunned. "What paper?"

"The annulment paper!"

Tito was taken back, not so much by the news as by Juanita's anger. She had consistently maintained that he could get out of the counterfeit marriage at any time. Yet she was obviously vexed by the arrival of the legal paper.

"Let's take a walk."

"I've got work to do. I can't . . ."

But he reached out and took her by the wrist. Then he led her out of the house. He saw where the boys were working and turned the opposite way. The path led out to a point of sorts, the last high ground before the land sloped down toward the creek.

"You don't have to explain," she said to his back. "I never expected you to continue the pretense of a marriage. You've been more than honorable about this entire affair."

He rotated around to see her staring at the ground in front of her feet. "Juanita, I—"

"We will leave as soon as we can. It's just that I don't know where to go now."

"Go?" He was dumbfounded. "What do you mean, go?"

She lifted her head and he could see the tears glistening in her eyes. "We won't be a burden to you, Mr. Pacheco. I only wanted to escape Ivory Flats with my family intact. Judge Lockard would have found homes for the children. We would have been split up— possibly for the rest of our lives. At least now, I will make sure we stay together as one family."

"You're not going anywhere," he told her flatly. "This is your new home."

Juanita showed a perplexed look. "What do you mean?"

"My name is on the claim, but I was going to let this homestead go back to the recorder's office. With my job, I don't have time to improve the land and such. I'm sure with you and the boys here, we can make a go of it.''

"I don't understand.''

"Juanita, I brought you here to stay, you and the kids. It isn't much, but it's better than nothing.'' At her continued frown, he hurried on. "Besides, once we have a deed, it'll be a real home.''

"You expect us to stay here in Broken Spoke?''

"Of course. I wouldn't have brought you all the way to Wyoming to then be rid of you. You needed a home for the kids and this is all I had to offer.''

"But the annulment papers . . .''

"Judge Lockard told me he was going to send the document to Broken Spoke. He figured one week would be enough to get you settled in. It's me who isn't going to hold you to a pretense marriage. You did what you had to do.''

"You spoke to the judge?'' She tossed her hair with a rather vigorous shake of her head. "You mean you could have put an end to this hoax at any time?''

Tito squirmed under her hard stare. "Yes, Judge Lockard made it clear the marriage was only temporary, so the town fathers wouldn't start splitting up you and the kids.''

"But you continued with the ruse! Why did you stay with us? bring us here to . . .'' She appeared to grope for the right words. "What about these people in Broken Spoke? You've already introduced me around town as your wife!''

"Don't worry about it. We can work something out.''

"Work something out?'' She was incredulous.

"We're talking about me calling myself Mrs. Pacheco! The annulment paper has changed all of that."

He shook his head. "Nothing has changed."

"Tito! You're not making sense!"

"For the time being, let's pretend the paper didn't arrive," he suggested. "Those killers are bound to show up any day. As far as anyone in town is concerned, you're my wife. If something should happen to me, this place and everything I own will pass on to you and the kids. That's fine with me. I don't have much, but you are welcome to it."

"I'm not going to think of anything bad happening to you. If you don't mind, I'd as soon keep my family together without your getting killed!"

"I'm only saying we shouldn't make any decisions until this is over between me and Puggot. Leave things as they are for the next little while. Once he is out of our lives, we can decide how to proceed."

"But, Tito, how am I supposed to act? How do I behave? Am I still Mrs. Pacheco or do I start correcting people? The longer this charade lasts, the harder it is going to be to ever unscramble it."

"You don't have to do or say anything right now. Let's go to the dance. We could both use a little fun."

"What about your friends? What are they going to think?"

He smiled at her. "They'll think I've got the prettiest gal at the ball."

"You know what I meant."

"And I meant what I said, you'll be the prettiest girl there."

Juanita blushed appropriately. "I've only got one nice dress—the one you bought for me."

"It'll do just fine."

She showed him a slight smile. "All right, Tito. I'd love to go to the dance with you."

Chapter Sixteen

Cully had followed Joe for most of the afternoon without saying a word. It had been an uneventful search, riding a wide circle to make sure Puggot's band had not entered the valley. Cole and Bunion were watching town, and all of the ranchers were on alert. The purpose of his and Joe's vigilance was to insure the gang had not slipped by unseen. Darkness was covering the land when Joe stopped at the Dakota Creek to water the animals. The two of them dismounted before Joe broke the silence.

"I have the feeling that you are with me in body, Cully Deeks, but not in spirit."

"The dance will be starting in a little while and I'm leaving the door open to all the other bachelors in the valley, Joe. Amber is going to be the target of a dozen guys, plus that sweet-talker, Darby. I feel like I'm going to lose my shot, you know?"

Joe grunted. "You believe she is your one and only love?"

"I've never been bit by the passion bug before, but I've got me a full dose this go-round."

"If the lady feels the same way, you shouldn't have to worry about her dancing with another gentleman or two."

"Yeah, but it tears at my guts, Joe, thinking she might be smiling at another guy, that she might be in someone's arms, even if it is only dancing. Is that part of love?"

"Love is an invisible force with which a man can move a mountain."

"Gal durn, if you ain't about the smartest-talking man I ever come across—white or otherwise."

"I read a good many books. There is no such thing as a really smart man, my friend, for the more a person learns in this world, the more he realizes his own ignorance."

"So what about my problem, Joe. Should a man hate to see his woman talk or smile at another man?"

"I believe most forms of jealousy can be defined as the insecurity of the relationship between a man and woman. If you are convinced of the devotion the other person has for you, you will see the smile or talking as only idle conversation or being polite. If you are insecure, you might view the same action as a potential threat to your relationship."

"Well, I expect I'm jealous 'cause I got good reason. Amber ain't never made me no promises."

"Have you asked for any commitment?"

"Not exactly."

"And have you been actively courting the lady?"

"Kind of."

"By kind of, does that mean taking her for an afternoon ride, going on an outing or two together, or sitting by her at the Sunday meetings?"

Cully ducked his head. "I ain't had so much time lately, and I kind of missed the last couple Sundays."

"I would venture you have cause to worry," Joe

quipped. "How do you expect to win the fair maiden, when you are never there to demonstrate your affection?"

"I know, I know, but . . ." He shrugged his shoulders. "I ain't much for this pursuing thing. I never had to go out and try to impress a gal before. If you were me, how would you go about it?"

"Two options come to mind."

"Yeah?"

"You could take by a couple of good horses as presents to show the Ingersol family you are a worthwhile man and serious about winning the lady's hand. Or try camping in front of her door until the family tosses out her clothes."

Cully frowned. "What kind of romance is that?"

"Indian romance, depending on your tribe."

"I belong to the white tribe, Joe. We don't have no rituals like that."

"Too bad. I know where I could have picked you up a couple of fine horses at a real good price."

"Like I said, you're a smart cuss for an Indian."

"Compared to some of you white men, I am closer to the genius level."

Cully chuckled. "I expect I'm among those."

"A man's intellect is limited only by his learning ability and willingness to put forth the effort, Cully Deeks. When it comes to women, I don't believe any man is smart enough to understand them completely."

"So what's the answer?"

"As I stated, it's the effort a man puts forth. If you actively aspire to endear the girl to you, it will make the difference between ending up with a warm lodge and happy home, rather than having to settle for a cold camp and a thrown-together lean-to.''

''I expect you're right.''

''Naturally.''

''You ever do any courting of your own, Joe? I mean, did you ever have some little maiden stir your heart?''

Joe was quiet for a moment, staring off into space. Cully had about decided he hadn't heard the question, when Joe began to speak.

''I remember the soft outline of her petite features, the way the light would dance on her raven hair. She had the voice of an angel and often sang softly to herself. I first saw her at a mountain stream.

''There were fish in the pools, and I was collecting enough for a meal. I happened around a bend in the creek and she was on her knees on the bank, washing clothes and singing. I have never heard or seen such a vision since.''

''Did you speak to her?''

''She was an Arapaho, hated enemy of the Shoshone. I surprised her, but she did not run away. To the contrary, she stared back at me with the most beautiful eyes I have ever seen. I told her not to be frightened and she laughed.'' He smiled at the memory. ''I suppose I didn't look to pose any threat, standing with fish in one hand and a pole in the other.''

''So what happened?''

''I said hello.''

''And?''

''Her mother appeared, charged in like a black-backed bison bull—about the same size too. The earth shook when she walked, each step like claps of thunder. She waved a fist at me and warned me to stay away from her daughter.''

"What did you do?"

"The mother is the mold for the daughter. I realized what the maiden would look like in ten years. I must confess, it was a sobering vision."

"I understand you."

"As for you, I suggest you start—" He stopped speaking and lifted his head. Suddenly, he held up his hand for silence.

Cully had heard it too, the sound of pounding hooves. Both of them moved to cover the nose of their own pony, so the animals would do no "howdying" to the passing horses. It was dark enough that the riders were only shadows against the dusk.

"Four men," Cully whispered. "You think it's them?"

"Riding toward town," Joe surmised, looking after them. "It could be about anyone looking for someplace to spend Saturday night. They may even know there is a dance at Cartwell's saloon tonight."

"We could follow them and see what they're up to. What do you think?"

Joe gave his head a negative shake. "My vote would be to keep up the search. There are only four men in that group, and they are headed into Broken Spoke. Mallory and the others will be watching any new arrivals in town."

"Might only be a coincidence," Cully said, "but I didn't recognize any of those four men."

"Little too dark to see them clearly, but their horses were packing a lot of dust. They could have come from a long way off."

"What now?"

"Let's stick to the plan and keep looking. Now that we have the cover of darkness, we can make our way along the main roads."

"We going to stay out all night?"

"No, I told Mallory we'd meet him at his place around midnight. We have time to check the main trails and still get there by then."

"I guess that means we eat in the saddle," Cully said, as he stuck a foot into the stirrup and mounted his horse. "Next time, I ain't going to volunteer for nothing."

There were several new faces at the dance, but that was normal. With people traveling through town and the stage often staying over on Saturday nights, there were usually a few unfamiliar faces around. Luke and Tito spent a portion of the night trying to take note of anyone who seemed inordinately interested in asking questions or watching from a distance. However, Tito had brought Juanita to the dance, and Luke spent time with Timony, so neither had time to really observe each and every man at the gathering.

After a slow dance, Luke and Tito took their girls over to join John Fairbourn and Cassandra, the woman he was courting. The three ladies were left standing together, while the men took a walk around the saloon, to check new faces.

Timony grew tired of the awkward silence and started a conversation with the other two. "This is about as uncouth as dancing on stilts," she complained. "I spend every second looking over Luke's shoulder, watching for someone with a gun."

"It does dampen the spirit of the evening," Cassie agreed.

"How are you holding up, Mrs. Pacheco?" Timony asked. "Tito has been a bachelor for so long, do you have him housebroken yet?"

Juanita flushed at the question. "I'm not used to being called Mrs. Pacheco yet. In fact, I don't know exactly what kind of relationship Tito and I have. I'm sure both of you know the truth by now, that the marriage was a ruse to gain a name, so I could keep my family together."

"The way Tito was holding you on the dance floor," Cassie observed, "I don't think he wants to put an end to the ruse."

"He is a very honorable man."

"It appeared to be more than honor," Timony remarked, watching Juanita's expression. "Is there some chance that the two of you are going to make this a real marriage?"

The girl blushed again. "I-I don't know."

"You could do worse," Cassie said. "John thinks very highly of Tito. I respect his opinion in about everything."

"I agree," Timony joined in, "my brother is a very good judge of character."

"You don't understand," Juanita murmured softly. "I tricked Tito into the marriage. How can I tell if he really likes and wants me, or if he is only being a decent man?"

Cassie smiled. "I've seen him looking at you, Juanita. I think it's pretty evident the man has developed deep feelings for you."

"How can you be so sure?"

"I loved John before we ever exchanged more than a passing word," she answered solemnly. "I had been forced into a marriage I didn't want, wed to a man I could not even respect. When John first gazed into my eyes, I knew he was the man I wanted to be with. We didn't have to say the words, it was like a strange kind of magic."

"I felt the same thing toward Luke," Timony admitted. "And I really had to work hard for him. He kept putting his job first and that really hurt."

Juanita shook her head. "I don't understand. What if he only desires to be with me? How is a person supposed to know the difference between physical lust and true love?"

Timony took a deep breath and let it out slowly. "I believe that lust is only a desire to possess someone, while love is sharing and showing consideration for another person's feelings. Lust will burn out when the physical desire is satisfied, but love grows over a period of time."

"Well stated, Timony," Cassie put in. "Love is a faith you put in someone, the faith that they will always be there for you."

The three men returned to stop any further discussion about eternal commitment. Each of the women moved to the side of her respective man. Timony put her arm around Luke's waist, while Cassie slipped her arm into the crook of John's own. Juanita only hesitated a moment before she joined hands with Tito. It was such a natural act, he seemed not even to notice the touch of color it brought to her cheeks.

John spoke first. "Must be a dozen new faces in town. If I was going to pick out a couple to watch, it would be the two next to the door, the big man and the dude.''

Luke's head bobbed in agreement. "They look to have traveled a few miles."

"I don't know." Tito was not convinced. "From the information I've picked up about the gang, no one said anything about some dandy riding with Puggot. The guy by the door is wearing a fifty-dollar suit, a new Stetson, and very expensive boots. He doesn't fit into a gang of cutthroats."

"They've been doing the most observing," Luke argued. "Take a gander at how they keep watching Darby."

"They might only be checking out Amber Ingersol," Timony suggested. "She's quite striking in that yellow and white Princess Polonaise dress."

"I'm impressed, Timony," Cassie said. "I didn't know you were so informed about fashion."

"That type of dress was featured in *Harper's Bazaar* some time back. I read how it had been dubbed the Dolly Varden."

"I used to subscribe to that magazine!" Cassie exclaimed.

"And you don't anymore?"

"When I came to Wyoming, it was something left behind. I do miss it."

"I'll bring over some back issues," Timony volunteered. "You know what I really like is the articles about new inventions and such. Did you see where they actually have electric streetcars in New York?"

Before the conversation could continue, Luke jumped in. "Hey, they are playing another slow tune. The night isn't getting any younger." He rotated around and took up a dancing position with Timony. As the music filled the room, he and she began to dance into the crowd.

John and Cassandra were next to join the dancers. Tito stood only for another moment, before he turned to Juanita. "Shall we?"

She smiled. "The way I keep stepping on your feet, I would think you'd prefer to watch. Are you sure you'll be able to walk tomorrow?"

"Practice is all it takes, my dear," he said lightly. "Before the night is over, we'll be demanding they play a tango for the two of us."

"Only in your dreams, Tito," she scoffed. "I saw a couple perform one of those at a carnival once. I'm not going to let you throw me around like a rag doll."

"That was not the kind of tango I had in mind."

"Whatever, let's stick to these slow tunes, where I only step on your toes."

Chapter Seventeen

Domino nudged Swede in the ribs. "You hear the girl in the yellow dress? She called her partner Darby. He's the one."

"There are a half-dozen Mexicans in the room," Swede answered. "Which one do you think is Tito Pacheco?"

"It won't matter. I've got an idea for a plan. Baxter wanted us to locate the two gents who killed Saul, but we can have them come to us instead."

"I'm in favor of any kind of a plan that figures how to cut the odds. I see no less than twenty fighting men in this room. If Pacheco has friends, we could be in for a full-scale war."

"Like I said, we'll make Darby and Tito come to us."

"Yeah? And how do we do that?"

"Slip word to Trapper and Haynes to ease out and meet at the horses. Once we get out of here, I'll explain it for you."

"Sounds good to me. Standing here, I feel like I've got a target painted on my forehead."

Domino grinned. "We won't have any trouble getting those two men now, Swede. This job is going to be short and sweet."

* * *

The single lamp shown from the Ingersol farmhouse before Donny spoke up. "Dang, if you wasn't about as popular as the only flower in a hive of bees, Sis. I'll bet you didn't hardly get to sit down a full dance tune all night."

Amber smiled, thinking of how Darby had fussed over her all night. There had been another two or three men who kept cutting in or asking her to dance too. Never had she so thoroughly enjoyed being confined in petticoats and a dress.

"It's a good thing your beau, Deeks, wasn't there," Ray added. "He'd have been butting heads with every one of those gents."

"Where was Deeks anyway?" Donny wanted to know.

"Cully had to ride night guard with Injun Joe. They are worried that those bounty hunters will come to Broken Spoke."

"Yeah, I remember the talk about those boys at the meeting. I can't imagine them trying to come into this town and making a show of force. We've got more than enough guns ready to stop them."

"I hope they never show up," Amber said. "I wouldn't want you two getting into a gunfight or something."

"Donny could knock them off at five hundred yards," Ray bragged. "He's about the best shot with a rifle there is."

"And we've got Mallory, the Indian, the ranchers, and a bunch more. They'd be real stupid to come in gunning for Tito and Darby here in Broken Spoke."

"So which one do you like best?" Ray asked Amber, returning to the original subject.

"I like them both."

"I seen Darby holding your hand between dances," Donny teased. "You didn't look like you wanted to be shed of him."

"He's a very polite young man."

"Looks like Ma is still up," Ray said. "Guess she was worried we might get lost in the dark."

Donny pulled up in front of the house. "I'll put up the wagon. You two go ahead and get ready for bed."

"No argument from me," Ray said.

Amber found a foothold and climbed down first. She had barely set foot on the ground when the door opened. It wasn't her mother, however, who was framed against the light, but two men with guns!

"Rest easy, all of you!" the one snapped.

Another man came out of the dark on the opposite side of the wagon. "Do as Trapper says!"

Before Donny or Ray had a chance to do anything, there were four men, all with guns trained on them.

"What's the deal here?" Donny asked. "Who are you? What do you want?"

"You shut your yap, sonny!" the man called Trapper spoke harshly. "One wrong word and we'll cut you all down like so many stalks of corn."

"What have you done to our ma?" Amber demanded to know. "Is she all right?"

"No one is going to get hurt," he answered, "lessen' one of you gets cute."

"She's kind of cute already, Trapper," the man next to him said, showing his tobacco-stained teeth.

"All of you come into the house," Trapper said,

ignoring the comment. "You boys leave your guns on the wagon."

"And don't be thinking of trying nothing," one of the men warned from the other side.

Donny and Ray had no choice but to unhitch their guns and climb down. Once on the ground, they were herded into the house. Edna was sitting in her rocking chair, apparently unharmed, scowling at the intruders.

"You boys sit on the floor with your backs to the wall," Baxter directed them. "As for you, young lady"—he shifted his attention to Amber—"you get on some riding duds."

"What for?" Ray challenged. "She ain't going nowhere with you!"

One of the men used his gun and clubbed Ray from behind. The blow stunned him, but it was not a hard enough blow to knock him unconscious. He was shoved to the floor, where he put a hand up to rub the back of his head.

"Like I says," Trapper proclaimed, "no one gets hurt—not the girl here, not no one—so long as you do what you're told."

"Do what the blowhard tells you to, kids," Edna spoke up. "We ain't got no choice."

"She's right," Trapper repeated, "you ain't got no choice." He waved his gun at Amber. "Get some riding clothes on, right quick."

She hurried into the sectioned-off bedroom and began to change clothes. Her fingers trembled with the buttons and her heart was thundering in her chest. She couldn't imagine what these men wanted with her. They had to be the gang who had come for Tito and Darby, but why come to their house?

To her relief, they allowed her to change her clothes in private. She threw on a riding skirt and wool blouse, added a jacket for warmth, then pulled on her boots. Lastly, she picked up her riding hat, buckskin gloves, and a winter scarf. When she returned to the main room, she saw that one of her two brothers was missing.

"Where is Donny?" she asked.

"He's okay, Sis." Ray was the one to answer. "They sent him to fetch Tito and Darby. That's what all this is about."

"Let's go, lady," Trapper ordered. Then he swept his gun around the room. "You two do as you're told and none of you will come to harm." He met Edna's cold stare. "I mean what I say, woman. We don't have no fight with you and your kids. This here ain't no kidnapping, it's insurance that the two murdering scum who killed Saul Puggot and Quint Avery will come alone."

"So you can kill them in cold blood!" Ray retorted. "And you call them murdering scum?"

"It ain't open for discussion, bub. If your brother sends those two sidewinders to us, we'll turn your sister loose and she'll be on her way. It's that simple."

Ray had no reply. Edna looked very worried, but she said nothing. Amber was hustled out the door and put on a horse. Within seconds, she and several men were riding back down the trail into the pitch black of the night.

Tito dropped Luke off at his place and it left him and Juanita alone. They had already been out to the Fairbourn ranch to return Timony home. Luke gave a farewell wave and Tito headed the team back toward the creek crossing and his own spread.

"It was nice to spend time with your friend, Mr. Mallory. He seems very nice, and I really like Timony."

"I know your family will like it here."

For some reason, Juanita became withdrawn. Tito moved the carriage along until they crossed the Dakota Creek. He glanced at her a couple of times, but she had her head turned, constantly looking away from him. Something had struck a discordant note and he wasn't sure what. He decided not to ruin a pleasant evening.

"Something bothering you, Juanita?"

"No."

"You sure?"

"I'm sure it's nothing to concern you."

"What are you talking about?"

"My family—you said that my family would like it here. I forgot for a moment that you are not part of our family."

The lamp burned suddenly brighter in his brain. "I didn't mean for it to sound like that."

"It's my fault. I keep thinking of you as being . . ." She broke off. "I'm sorry. I have no right to have such misguided thoughts."

He let the horse make its way across the creek and climb the hill. When the cabin was in sight, he pulled back on the reins and stopped the buggy. Turning to look at the girl, he could only partly make her out in the darkness. "Listen, Juanita. I don't want you feeling there is a need for pretense between us."

"What choice do I have? I had the judge trick you

into a phony marriage. I only wanted a name, to be in a legal position to assume responsibility for my brothers and sisters. It was a selfish and underhanded act on my part. I was desperate. I did what I felt I had to do, but I haven't the right to make demands on you, or expect you to think of us as your real family. Now that you have the annulment, I don't know what to think.''

"It isn't any easier for me!" He tried to demonstrate the opposite viewpoint. "I feel like I'm caught between the bull and the fence here. I don't know what's expected of me. Am I to forget that we are sort of married, or do I court you like I would any other girl? How do I know if we even like each other?''

"Of course, we like each other," she murmured. "Or, at least, I like you.''

"So, what am I supposed to do, Juanita? I took particular care not to take advantage of our . . . arrangement.''

"Advantage?''

He sighed, deciding it was time to clear the air between them. "I'm ten years older than you, Juanita. I've been everything from a drifter to a hired gun. I've killed men in war and in fights where I had no choice. I can't expect you to want to be tied down to someone of my background, or even with our age difference.''

"I'm fully grown, Tito. I've had to be responsible for my younger brothers and sisters most of my life. I could not accept a boy or immature man as my husband. I . . .'' She lowered her head demurely. "I would prefer someone like you.''

"But I've nothing to offer a family but days or even weeks at a time of being gone. With a band of killers after my hide, I might even be killed. I don't want to leave you alone to raise your brothers and sisters, but it could happen.''

''It won't.''

''How can you be so sure?''

''I just am.''

''You're not only sneaky, but you are headstrong, young lady.''

She smiled. ''I suppose, when I have to be.''

''So where does that leave us?''

''We never said the actual words, Tito,'' she whispered. ''When you and I sign the papers Judge Lockard sent, the marriage will be annulled. I won't hold you to any matrimonial promises and you don't owe us anything. Giving us a home of our own is more than I could have hoped for.''

''Yes, but what if we decide to keep the marriage going?''

She lifted her head and stared at him. He could perceive a gentle expression on her face, her lips slightly pursed, as if she was holding her breath.

''Would you like that, Tito? I mean, would you really want to be burdened with such a large family?''

''Well, I'll admit, I feel a little cheated. I mean, the only kiss I got was one I wasn't prepared for, and I never did get the chance to rehearse the part where the preacher is supposed to say to have and to hold.''

Juanita leaned in his direction until he slipped an arm around her shoulders. ''You mean like this?'' she asked.

He drew her in against him. ''Yes, this feels right, like it was meant to be.''

Her head lifted as she rotated around to look up at him. "I think it was meant to be too, Tito."

"You mean you would really marry a man like me, for real?"

She didn't answer, but rose up to press her lips against his. He held her tightly in his arms, wishing the moment could last forever. It did linger for a few seconds, until the sound of a horse reached their ears.

They broke at once and Tito quickly drew his gun.

"Pacheco!" the man called out. "It's Don Ingersol! There's trouble!"

Chapter Eighteen

Luke was pouring coffee for Joe and Cully when the riders came boiling over the hill and into the yard. Joe looked out the single window and whistled.

"Those fellows are looking to take a bite out of Mother Earth and having horses with broken legs. Not a smart idea, riding so hard in the dark!"

"Something is up." Cully spoke the obvious. "Who is it?"

Luke opened the door as Don and Tito came to jarring stops, skidding to a halt right in front of the front of the house.

"What's the hurry, Tito? You tired of living?"

"They're here!" he said breathlessly. "Don says they took his sister to guarantee what they want. They expect Darby and I to ride out alone and meet them."

"They took Amber?" Cully shouted. "How? When?"

"Be suicide," Joe piped up. "We spotted their camp an hour ago. There were five of them at the fork in the road, two miles outside of town. They had put on coffee and looked to be waiting for someone or something."

"There were four men waiting for us at our place," Don told them. "They sent me to bring you the word.

Unless you agree to meet them alone, at sunup in the morning, they'll send Amber home in a box.''

"Meet them where?" Luke asked.

"Right where the Indian just said, at the main fork north of town.''

Luke looked at the Indian. "And you counted five men?''

"It's a good possibility they had already split up. We saw a few riders going into Broken Spoke around dusk. They could have been from the same bunch. If the four at the Ingersol place were separate from the main group, that would give Puggot's bunch a total of nine men.''

"What about my sister?" Donny wanted to know.

"We'll do exactly as they said," Tito replied. "We won't let them hurt Amber.''

"But you and Darby wouldn't stand a chance against them alone!" Luke argued. "We have to have a plan, some way to even the odds.''

"I'm open to suggestions, Luke, but I won't be responsible for those men doing any harm to Amber.''

Luke turned to Joe. "What about the layout at the fork?" he asked. "How close did you get? Is there cover for us to get within shooting distance?''

"We used the drainage ditch that winds along the main trial," Cully explained. "We left our horses down in a glen and sneaked and crawled on our bellies for a quarter mile or so. It only got us as close as maybe three hundred yards.''

"Closer to four," Joe corrected. "Wouldn't be much of a shot for a buffalo hunter. Any of you have a fifty-caliber rifle tucked away?''

"My Winchester will reach that far, but not with much accuracy," Cully said.

Donny shrugged. "I'm pretty good with a rifle, but we're not talking about men out in the open. I recollect there are some boulders and an old dead tree right at the fork. Those boys will have cover."

"What if we get everyone in town and swoop down on them?"

"They might hurt Amber," Luke said in answer to Cully's offer. "Plus, we could get a dozen people killed."

"Then we do as they ask," Tito said. "Darby and I will ride down alone."

"Suicide," Joe told him.

"Nine of them against two of you—what chance would you have?" Donny also was not enthusiastic about the notion. "Got to be another way."

Luke was turning the ideas over in his head. The others looked at him for his input. After a moment, he surveyed the group. "Maybe it isn't a bad idea after all."

"What?" Cully couldn't believe it. "Tito and Darby will be gunned down like mad dogs!"

"You crazy, Mallory?" Donny was also incredulous. "I thought Tito was your friend!"

"Hear me out, boys," Luke said. "This might work."

In a riding skirt and with her hair down, Amber looked the part of a genteel young lady. For that reason, the group of rowdies didn't bother to tie her hands. They assumed her to be no threat to escape. The one called Nolen saw her to comfort, giving her a blanket to sit on and a second to keep around her shoulders for warmth.

Amber kept her eyes moving, evaluating the gang members, considering her options. She knew her brothers would bring help. There would be a plan of some kind, and she would have to be ready to make the most of an escape attempt. She was not the helpless female she appeared. Amber had grow up as a tomboy her entire life, up until she came to Broken Spoke. She had wrestled and fought with her brothers and anyone else who wanted to cross paths with her. She was pretty strong and very fleet afoot, able to outrun both Donny and Ray. She also knew to hit with her wrist locked, so she wouldn't injure herself. Lastly, she was keenly aware that a weapon was better than a bare fist.

Sitting quietly, she discreetly gathered several small rocks. To anyone paying attention, she appeared to be occupying her time by mindlessly toying with a few harmless stones. However, she had her buckskin riding gloves in her hands. Ray had purchased them for her as more of a joke than anything else. He teased her, saying she would have to learn to ride sidesaddle, wear a woman's jockey-style hat, and would need the gloves to protect her dainty fingers from the rough grip of the saddle horn. Carefully, she fed a stone and some sand into the glove and shoved it to one of the finger-tips. Then she repeated the act, over and over, until the glove had four fully loaded fingers and was stuffed with a pound or more of rock and sand.

"Would you like some coffee, ma'am?" Nolen suddenly asked.

Amber about let out a shriek from the surprise. She

instantly recovered and gave her head a negative shake.

"No one is going to touch you, ma'am," Nolen said. "I swear it."

She looked up and could see the man was deadly serious. "Thank you for the comforting words, sir. I am a little terrified by all of this."

Guilt flooded his features. "It's only so no innocent parties get hurt, ma'am. Mr. Puggot only wants to get to the men who killed his brother. We've no fight with the people of Broken Spoke."

She took a look around. "I see he is interested in it being a fair fight, with only nine men to go up against two. How brave and tough you all must feel."

"We know Pacheco has friends here. We had to bring enough men to force him out into the open."

"Then you'll shoot him down without giving him a chance," she stated. "No wonder you kidnapped me. It would be unthinkable if you had to face an equal number of men from town."

"Nolen!" Baxter snarled. "Tell the hussy to shut her yap, or I'll stuff a sock between her teeth and she can suck on it all night!"

Amber recoiled appropriately to appear frightened by his threat. She had to lull the group into thinking she was weak, frail, and too timid to make any attempt at escape. Surprise would be necessary if she were to have any chance of getting away.

Nolen, however, came to her defense. "If something were to happen to this lady, we'll be the ones with our names on wanted posters, Bax. I ain't going to let that happen."

"We got everything covered here. Soon as them

two jaspers show up, we'll turn her loose. I told you before, we didn't kidnap her, we are using her to insure those two come to face us.''

"Then what?" he shot back. "We have four to their one. That'll be like murder, if we open fire on two men. We could still wind up on a circular for murder."

"Danged if you don't sound yella' to me, Nolen!"

"He has a point," Walt spoke up. "Nine against two won't look good."

"Are you boys with me or not?" Baxter snarled the words. "I don't want a bunch of yella' coyotes backing my play."

Walk wilted at once. "No need to get insulting, Bax. I'm just saying how it could look."

"They kilt my brother," Baxter said, suddenly saddened by the memory. "He was only a kid, a big, lovable kid. I raised that boy, ever since our ma died. He was like my shadow, following me around, wanting to be just like his older brother. I always looked out for him. I was responsible for him. That's why I didn't bring him into our gang, 'cause I was worried he would get hurt."

"We all know how you felt about Saul," Chiggers said. "And we'll back you up against his killers."

"That's right," Marx added. "We'll see them two dying in their own blood."

Baxter mellowed. "Thanks, boys. I knew I could count on you."

Amber listened and watched. She studied each man, trying to determine if he had a weakness she could exploit. After a while, she knew Nolen was the one with the most conscience. But he was also the one least trusted by Baxter. As the night progressed, there were always two men on guard. It was impossible for her to outmaneuver both at once time. Any attempt at getting away would have been futile. Finally, she closed her eyes and tried to rest. Come daylight, she would study the options again and watch for a chance to escape.

Joe led the way, so quiet Luke could not hear him moving. He and the two Ingersol boys followed along in the dark. John, Billy, Token, and Cully Deeks were on the opposite side of the valley, making a circle. They would come up the road from behind the group of bounty hunters. The old marshal, Jack Cole, Bunion, Cartwell, and a half-dozen farmers and ranchers were going to back Tito and Darby. In all, they would have more than twenty guns in the field against Puggot's men.

However, it was not a fight they were looking for, but a way to prevent a war. Luke didn't want to get a dozen people killed. Tito had suggested the final action, the only way to end the battle without a lot of bloodshed on both sides. Luke and the others were only a means to that end.

"This is as far as we can go," Joe whispered. "The wash bellies out to nothing in another fifty feet."

The four of them settled down, their rifles ready, lying on their stomachs, waiting for the sun to cast the first light over the eastern sky. Donny was at Luke's left shoulder, the Indian to his right, with Ray a few feet away.

"Can't hardly see that far," Donny said. "We can't shoot with my sister in among them."

"They said they would release her, once Tito and

Darby showed up alone. We'll have to wait and hope they don't see the others.''

"Our best bet is to watch Amber," Donny replied. "She'll make a move of her own, first chance she gets. We have to be ready to cover her escape."

"You think she'd try to escape from nine men?" Luke was incredulous. "They have horses, you know."

"But they will be tethered on a picket line for the night. If my sis gets an opening, and figures which way to run, she'll make a break." He grinned at Luke. "And she's about as fleet afoot as a spooked deer. I'm pretty fast, but she can leave me in her dust. She's always been about the fastest runner I ever seen."

"It would give us some leverage, if she could manage it."

"We only got to watch. If they turn their back for a second, she'll be out of there like she was shot from a cannon."

Joe had been listening. "By the time the sun comes up, I'll be in a position to show her which way to run."

"How can you do that?"

Joe pulled a piece of glass from his pocket. "I'll use an old Indian trick the white man stole from us, signaling with a mirror."

"We stole it from you?" Luke whispered. "Since when did Indians invent the mirror?"

"Quiet down, white eyes," Joe retorted. "You want those guys out there to know we're here?"

Chapter Nineteen

At the edge of town, Tito sat in the borrowed buggy. Juanita was snuggled up to him, both of them under a single blanket.

"You shouldn't have come," Tito said, after a lengthy silence.

Juanita rose up and kissed him. "Do you really mean that?"

"If this doesn't work, I wouldn't want you to be here." He searched for the right words. "I mean, if I were kil—"

She placed a finger over his lips to stop the flow of words. "I love you, Tito," she murmured softly. "My place is at your side."

He took her into his arms and held her close. "I still can't believe this is real, Juanita. When you consider the incredible turn of events it took for us to end up together, it's a wonder we ever even met."

"Destiny, my dear Tito, it was our destiny."

"I'm beginning to think my destiny has always been at Broken Spoke," he said. "I want you to be a part of it, for the rest of my life."

She again lifted her head and kissed him. "I promise"—she breathed the words next to his ear—"to have and to hold, from this day forward."

173

"And I do too," he responded in turn, holding her tight.

Together, they watched as the first rays of light began to bring the dark world into focus. Each knew these precious moments could be the beginning of a long and happy life together, or it could be the last twinkling they would ever share.

Darby had been waiting in the saloon. He came out to stand by the buggy. Tito could see the apprehension in his face, the terror behind his eyes. He had never faced death before, but he was a man. He had come to fight and maybe die.

Tito finally pushed the blanket aside, smiled a last time at Juanita, then kissed her lightly on the lips. "It's time."

Amber was only half-awake, tired and aching from being cramped on the ground under her blanket all night. She had not seen a chance for an escape, but that didn't mean she had given up. As she stretched out her legs to get circulation, something flashed in her eyes. She immediately glanced around at the group of men, cognizant of anyone who might be watching.

Coffee was on and they were moving around. A couple were tending to the horses, another was rolling up a blanket, two were at the fire, and three more were staring toward town. Nolen was closest, but he was busy cleaning his gun. No one was paying her any attention. It allowed her to raise her head slowly and search for the flash again.

Moments past and there was nothing. The men keeping watch were not blind. Whoever had tried to signal her had to be aware of all nine men. Only when the beacon would go unnoticed could he try again. She held her breath and waited, careful not to lift her head enough to draw any attention to herself.

It came a second time, the glint of sunlight, quickly flashed, right into her eyes. She saw where the sign had come from and about gasped out loud. It was less than a hundred yards away, a harmless-looking, single clump of sagebrush. There was not the slightest indication that a man could hide in such a place, but she knew different. Someone was there! He was signaling to her!

Staring in that direction, she guessed her brothers were beyond the innocent stand of brush, nearly a quarter-mile away. A glance told her that it would take a full ten seconds for a man to grab a horse from the picket line. If they swung up onto the animal bareback, they would be on her before she could get farther than the sagebrush. However, she reasoned the men out in the brush would have taken that into consideration. They would know how far she had to run and they would have a plan to protect her from any rider.

Amber began to breathe deeply, trying to muster her wind. She carefully stretched her legs, while her heart began to hammer wildly in her chest. Somehow, she knew the man would signal her again, when it was time to make her break. Tucking the glove into her dress pocket, she slowly rose up to her feet.

"Would you like some coffee?" Nolen was watching her.

"Maybe in a few minutes," she replied. "I'm stiff from sleeping on the ground. If it's all right, I'd like to walk around a little."

"Stay within the perimeter of the camp," he

warned. "Some of these boys don't know how to be gentle with a lady."

"I appreciate your concern, Mr. Nolen. You are most considerate."

"Nothing bad will happen to you," he said. "Once them two show up, you'll be free to go."

She nodded her head and took a couple steps to get her blood circulating. A quick appraisal showed all of the men in camp were wearing cowboy boots. She knew if she got the chance, she could outrun every one of them. Bolstering her strength and attempting to steady her nerves, she waited for the signal.

"Here they come!" one man called to the others.

A man at the front put a pair of field glasses to his eyes. "Only two of them. One is a Mexican and the other is the one we heard the girl call Darby. It's them, all right."

Puggot was on the alert. "Keep your eyes open!" he said with a snarl. "They might try something cute!"

The man with the glasses did a slow sweep of the horizon. "Don't see anything moving, no dust, no nothing."

"Chiggers!" Puggot directed, "you keep holt of the girl."

Amber remained to the sagebrush side of the camp and made him come to her. He took hold of her arm, but she made sure it was her left. Meanwhile, she grasped the glove in her pocket and waited for the signal.

Tito and Darby came forward until they were less than a hundred yards away. Then they stopped.

"Turn loose the girl!" Darby called to the group.

"Keep a-coming!" Puggot hollered back. "We ain't falling for no tricks."

Six men had rifles, all ready for use. Amber saw that it was obvious Puggot's men didn't intend to give Tito and Darby a chance. This wasn't going to be a fight, it was going to be an execution.

There it was! The flash of light!

Amber used the glove of rocks, swinging it like a fist of steel. It smacked Chiggers across the forehead and knocked him right off of his feet. As he slammed to the ground, Amber took off running full out toward the sagebrush.

"Hey!" someone shouted. "Get her!"

"She's getting away!" cried another.

Amber had never run so hard in her life. She lifted her skirt above her knees and raced as hard and fast as she could go. One or two of the men started after her, but she quickly put distance between herself and them.

"Dad blame!" she heard one of them shout behind her. "She's faster'n a scalded cat!"

"I'll get her!" called another.

As she strove to keep up the scorching pace, she knew the last one was grabbing up a horse. Another few steps and she heard the mount pounding after her.

"This way, Sis!" Donny rose up from his concealment, still a full two hundred yards away. "Come on!"

He looked no bigger than a poker chip. She couldn't believe they expected her to run that far without being caught from behind. The hooves were louder, the horse drawing closer with every bound. She was a fast runner, but even she could not outrun a horse. The animal was practically breathing down her neck!

All at once, the sagebrush rose up from the ground, right in her path of flight. A rifle muzzle was pointed right at her! "Go around, woman!" Indian Joe cried. "Get out of the way!"

She veered off to one side and Joe fired the weapon.

Amber didn't look back, but there was no longer any sound of a horse. Several more rifles opened up, mostly from where her brother was at. They were putting down a covering fire while she continued to race toward them.

Several shots came from the rear and a bullet kicked up dust near Amber's feet. She began to zigzag, trying to make it a harder shot.

"Run straight!" a voice commanded from behind. "I've got your back covered!"

Amber realized that Joe was following her. She bolted ahead, hearing him close the distance until he was almost pushing her from behind.

"Hurry up!" Joe kept after her. "I thought you were fast on your feet!"

"Try it," she gasped between gulps of air, "try it in a dress!"

Donny, Ray, and Luke Mallory were all on their feet now, each firing his rifle as fast as he could pull the trigger and jack in a fresh round. They kept up the barrage until Amber reached the ditch. No one had to tell her to get down. She dived into the gully like it was a pool of water and slid to the bottom of the wash. Then she rolled onto her back, puffing like a wind-broke horse.

Shots came after her then, slapping into the ground

or screaming off of a rock. Luke and the others ducked for cover and reloaded their guns.

"Supposing they charge us?" Donny asked.

"They won't have time," Luke replied. "Listen."

Other guns were being fired. It sounded like a full-scale war going on.

"That would be John and his group from over on the other side. Cole and the men from town will be on their way to back up Tito and Darby. There's no place for those bounty hunters to go."

"Think they'll run?"

"We want to settle this, not put it off until a later date," Luke answered. "It won't be long now."

Suddenly, the shooting stopped. After a moment, Luke and the others raised their heads to see what was going on.

Tito was standing up. He had given the signal to cease firing. One of the men from the bounty hunters also stood up in the open.

"It's time you acted like a man, Puggot," Tito challenged. "If you want to face me, I'm standing right here."

Darby stood up alongside Tito. "Same here, Puggot! You got the guts to take us on in a fair fight?"

There was some grumbling and cussing back and forth among the hunters. Finally, a big man stepped out from the group. "What about all these guns you brought with you? How do we know we can trust you?"

"Two of us against you and any man riding with you!" Tito hollered back. "When it's over, your boys can ride away. We've no fight with any of them."

There was more discussion among the group, but

finally, Puggot and the dude stepped out from cover. They each took a moment to check their guns, then they started forward.

Luke and the others moved toward the group, aligning themselves in a position to make certain no one decided to change the odds with a rifle. As they approached, it was obvious that six of the seven men were willing to let Puggot do his own fighting. The seventh man was holding a hand to his bloody shoulder. He had been the one Joe knocked from his horse.

As one, all of them turned to watch the coming battle.

Chapter Twenty

"This is it," Darby said, his voice quaking from nerves and fear. "I got to tell you, I've never done me much fighting with a gun."

"The dude is the fast gun," Tito surmised. "You have to take Puggot."

"He's killed a dozen men, Pard. I've never even shot a deer."

"Take your time, aim carefully, and put one bullet into his chest. Don't think about what I'm doing, about the guns going off, nothing but your target."

Darby took a deep breath and let it out. "Right, one shot is all it takes, one bullet fired with a degree of accuracy."

"We won't let them get too close. It'll give you an even chance against Puggot. He'll be faster on the draw than you, but he won't take time to aim. If he misses his first shot, you make sure of your own."

"Oh, fine! If he misses!"

"Concentrate!" Tito snapped. "You'll only get one chance. If he misses his first try, he'll take a split-second to aim the second round. You have to nail him with your first shot."

"What about you?" Darby asked. "That dude looks real handy. He's wearing two guns!"

"The Domino Kid," Tito told him. "He's a flashy sort, but he's never gone up against anyone good."

"Are you good?"

"Better than anyone gives me credit for." He allowed himself a half-smile. "Except for maybe Luke Mallory."

Puggot and Domino kept walking, trying to shorten the distance to twenty paces or less, a comfortable range for a handgun. They slowed down, resting their hands on the butts of their guns, walking in a crouch, ready to draw. Tito let them come until they were a hundred feet, then ninety . . . eighty . . .

"Now!" he commanded.

Domino wasn't fast—he was quick as a ray of sunlight! His two pistols came up in a blur, hammers cocked back, both guns thrust forward to blast away. The bullet went off from Tito's gun a microsecond before Domino's pair. Only the shock of the bullet impacting on his chest caused his aim to waver. He pulled the triggers again as Tito fired a second time.

Puggot also blasted away. Darby yelped in surprise, but he returned fire and Puggot's hat flew off of his head. The man hesitated, flicking his eyes up at the part in his hair. It gave time for Darby to shoot again.

More shots, then a total silence. The echo of gunfire still rang in everyone's ears, but not a whisper of air moved.

Puggot was on his knees, his gun dug into the earth to hold himself upright. His left hand was tight over his heart, attempting to stop his life's blood from seeping down his chest. Domino still had both guns gripped firmly in his fists. His eyes were open wide, but he was flat on his back and unable to see the cloudless sky overhead. He would never see anything again.

"Kilt my brother!" Puggot's voice rasped. "Yuh worthless buzzards! I'll . . ." He sagged down until his forehead was against the ground. "I'll see . . . see yuh . . . dead. I'll . . ." Then he pitched slowly forward, pushing his bulb nose into the powdery dust.

Darby was holding his side, where a bullet had torn a path along his ribs. The smoke still lingered from Tito's gun. He had put four slugs into Domino and still the man had kept firing.

"You okay?" Darby asked, staring at him in disbelief.

Tito slowly holstered his gun. "No," he said softly, then collapsed into a heap.

Cully was among the first to arrive after the shooting. Bunion hurried to join him, carrying his medical bag. He stopped to check Tito as two of Baxter's men came out to have a look.

"You boys lost!" Darby squeaked the words, still trembling from head to foot. "It was a fair fight and we won!"

Cully put a hand on his gun as Luke and Joe arrived to join them. "You boys seen it," he said to Baxter's men. "Far as we're concerned, this here fracas is over."

"I don't know about you, Nolen," the one bounty hunter said to the other, "but I never figured Saul was worth getting kilt over."

"You got that right, Trapper. I think we ought to take the horses and ride. It's a long way home."

"How about having your medico look over Marx?"

Trapper said. "It's only a flesh wound, but it has bled some."

"Soon as I get a chance," Bunion said.

"You boys sure you don't want to keep the fight going?" Luke asked. "We aren't of a mind to look over our shoulders for you down the road apiece."

"It's over," Nolen said. "Most of us never figured it was worth the effort anyway. Saul was a bully who got by on his brother's reputation. We'll pull out as soon as Marx gets bandaged up."

"He the only one hit?"

"Pretty rotten shooting all around," Trapper remarked.

"We were only trying to pin you down," Luke admitted. "We didn't want a bloodbath today."

Nolen nodded his head. "Sorry about grabbing the girl. We also didn't want a bloodbath."

"If any of you touched her," Cully warned savagely, "you'll all die here and now!"

"They didn't hurt me none," Amber said, having walked over with her brothers to join the group. "But I sure clouted the one named Chiggers."

"He's still seeing double," Nolen said, displaying a slight mirth. "You nailed him good."

"I'm not as helpless as I might appear."

Nolen grunted. "I believe that. You're quite a gal."

"She's that, all right," Cully told him, moving over to stand next to her. "You men got off lucky here today."

"We'll be getting our horses ready," Nolen replied. "Won't no one see us around Broken Spoke again."

"That's a fact," Trapper agreed.

Bunion had Tito taken by wagon to his place, then

took a minute to tend to Marx. Once he was patched up, the men from Puggot's gang mounted up and rode away. They left the two bodies and fifty dollars for the burial of Domino and Puggot.

"Not exactly the sentimental type," Luke remarked to Joe as they watched the group slowly disappear down the trail.

"We were lucky."

"I'm for getting back to work. I've got a house to finish."

"How about Tito?"

"He's rawhide tough. He'll make it."

"Okay, white eyes, I'll help you load the bodies and get them into town. Then you owe me a drink."

"Lemonade?" Luke asked. "You can join Timony and me at the saloon."

Joe shook his head. "Civilization." He said the word with distaste. "It'll be the ruination of mankind."

The first vision was of an angel. She had black hair and brilliant brown eyes, as soft and gentle as those of a fawn. She reached out and stroked Tito's face. Her touch was cool and moist. It took a moment to realize that she was using a damp cloth to mop his brow.

"If this is death, I can't imagine why I've been dreading it."

"You might have been killed, Tito."

It was amazing. The angel sounded exactly like Juanita. After a few seconds, he made her out clearly.

"You mean I wasn't?"

"Bunion removed a bullet from your shoulder. Plus,

you were hit in one leg and just below the hip and grazed in two more places. I thought you told me you were fast with a gun.''

"Domino was no slouch either."

"You had no right to take on that gunman. You have a responsibility to a family—my family."

"What about you?"

She leaned down and placed a kiss on his mouth. Then she arose and smiled down at him. "That's up to you. I'm perfectly happy being Mrs. Pacheco."

"Well, I'm not."

She frowned. "But I thought—"

"Not until you marry me for real," he went on quickly. "I want to hear you say the proper words, with a ring and the kiss and everything."

Instead of speaking again, Juanita leaned over and kissed him a second time. Tito decided that sometimes actions spoke louder than words—and it felt just fine.